Chelsea, Lyric and Kailee -
Enjoy!

Day-Day

Sequel to the Award-Winning *Chop, Chop*

Book Two

L.N. Cronk

Kingdom Bound '09

www.LNCronk.com

Front Cover Photography by Hugo Chang.
Back Cover Photography by Dana Spiropoulou.

Spanish translations provided by Vicki Oliver Krueger.

ISBN Number: 978-0-9820027-1-1
Library of Congress Control Number: 2008933005

Published by Rivulet Publishing
West Jefferson, NC, 28694, U.S.A.

For Aaron and Mahaley.

You were running a good race. Who cut in on you and kept you from obeying the truth? Galatians 5:7

Laci and I did not have a *typical* engagement. Four years of living on a college campus and watching couples all around me had taught me what a *typical* engagement was like. They usually go something like this:

1. Guy buys ring...
2. Guy proposes and "surprises" girl with ring...
3. Guy and girl hug and kiss (crying is optional)...
4. Girl sticks ring in faces of all of her girlfriends (squealing in delight is *not* optional).

Laci and I didn't do any of that (except for maybe step three). Our engagement went more like this:

1. Guy and girl suddenly find themselves reunited after over three years apart...
2. Guy and girl make all wedding plans while living four hours away from each other and trying to finish college...
3. Girl *insists* that she doesn't need a ring – the money should go toward more important things...
4. Guy is stupid enough to listen to girl regarding ring.

This is what I was thinking about as I drove around Scottsdale (five days before our wedding), looking for the house that Laci shared with her roommates. I'd never been to Scottsdale before and her street address wasn't showing up on my GPS so I finally had to call.

So much for surprising her.

"Hey, David!"

"Hey, Laci. Where are you at?"

"In my room...studying."

"Where exactly is that?" I asked.

"Where's what?"

"Your room."

"What do you mean?"

"I mean I drove four hours to see you and I can't find your house anywhere...I can't even find your road."

"*You're here?!*"

"I don't know where I am," I said.

"*Why are you here?*"

"I wanted to see you..."

"Is everything okay?"

"It would be if I could find your house..."

"Where are you?"

"I told you," I said. "I don't have any idea where I am."

"Well, what do you see?"

"I just drove by a Pizza Hut."

"You're not even close," she said. "Just go back to the Pizza Hut and wait for me. I'll be there in about ten minutes."

"Okay."

"Are you sure everything's alright?"

"Positive."

"Okay," she said. "I'll be right there."

I didn't even see her pull up because I was looking for her in the wrong direction. Before I knew it she was opening up the passenger door of my car and climbing in.

"What are you doing here?" she asked, smiling at me and giving me a big hug.

"I was going to try to spy on you – you know, make sure you didn't have some other guy on the side or anything..."

She rolled her eyes.

"Come on," she said. "Why are you here? Don't you have an exam tomorrow?"

Two actually...

"Are you hungry?" I asked, ignoring her.

"No," she said. "I already ate. Why are you here?"

"Can't I come see you if I want to? Aren't you glad to see me?"

"Of course I'm glad to see you," she said, grabbing my hand, "but I've lived here for *four* years and you've never come to see me before."

"I've been busy."

She rolled her eyes again.

"Have *you* had dinner?" she asked.

"I'm okay," I said. I hadn't had dinner, but my stomach wasn't feeling great.

How ridiculous is it to be nervous about proposing to someone you're all set to marry in five days?

"Can we go somewhere and talk?" I asked.

I saw a look of concern cross her face and I knew she still wasn't convinced that everything was alright.

"Sure," she said. "There's a nice park not too far from here."

We pulled out of the parking lot and she told me where to go.

"So I guess I'm never going to get to see your house," I said as we drove along.

"Trust me," she said, "you're not missing anything."

"You might feel differently after we get to Mexico."

"Have you found anything new worth looking at?" she asked. We'd been working with a real estate agent in Mexico City over the Internet. He'd found us a lot of houses that were close to the orphanage where Laci would be doing much of her work, but only about three of them were big enough and within our price range at the same time.

"No," I said. "I think it's going to come down to the one with all the trees in the front yard or that *pink* one."

"It's not pink," she said for the hundredth time. "Turn here."

We drove up a long, blacktop road until we reached the parking lot. Only two other cars were there.

We walked over to the swings and each sat down on one. A young couple pedaled into the parking lot and began securing their bikes to the back of their SUV. Not too far from the swings, another young couple pushed the merry-go-round as their little boy rode in a circle.

"Are you done with exams?" I asked.

"Just one more on Wednesday," she said, pushing off and starting to swing. Her class was graduating on Friday night, but she'd be at our rehearsal dinner instead of attending. "What about you?"

"I've got two tomorrow and one on Thursday," I said. My class was graduating on Saturday, but I'd be getting married that day instead of attending.

"You've got *TWO* exams tomorrow?" she asked, clearly appalled. "You should be back at school studying!"

I waved my hand at her dismissively.

"I'm serious, David! You've worked hard for *four years*. I don't think you need to be blowing off your exams!"

"I'll do fine," I said. I felt pretty ready anyway, plus I already had a job lined up. I doubted they were going to renege their offer just because I didn't ace an exam or two.

She stopped swinging.

"Something's wrong," she said.

"No," I said, standing up. I stood in front of her and took her hands in mine and pulled her up to me. "Nothing's wrong."

I hugged her tight and then kissed her.

"Do you know that we've hardly spent any time together?" I asked quietly.

She nodded.

"I just wanted to spend some time with you before we get married...okay?"

She nodded again, but I could still see doubt. I dropped one of her hands and tugged on the other one toward the walking trail that circled the park.

It was about a half of a mile long and by the time we got back to where we'd started the young couple and their kid were gone and it was almost dark. We sat down on the merry-go-round and Laci began pushing against the ground with her foot. We started to go around and around and after about three passes I started to feel dizzy so I lay down. That just made it worse.

"Stop!" I said. "I feel sick."

"Yeah, right," she said, pushing extra hard.

"Stop, Laci...I'm serious... I get motion sickness."

She dragged her foot on the ground until we stopped.

"You get motion sickness?"

I threw my arm over my eyes and nodded.

"How can I not know that about you?" she asked.

"See? I told you. We've hardly spent any time together."

She lay down next to me and put her head on my shoulder.

"I've known you forever," she said quietly.

"Is this thing still moving?"

"No."

"It feels like it is..."

"Do you want to go sit under that tree?" she asked and I nodded.

We walked over to the tree and I sat down. Laci sat in front of me and leaned back against me. I put my arms around her.

"You didn't get sick when we flew to Mexico, did you?" she asked. That had been almost eight years ago and I could tell she was trying to remember.

"No," I said. "It's just roller coasters and boats and stuff."

"And merry-go-rounds?"

"Apparently."

"So we're not going to an amusement park for our honeymoon?"

"No."

"Where are we going?"

"Nice try," I said, "but I'm going to have to be a whole lot sicker than this before I tell you that."

"Are we flying?"

"Of course we are," I said.

"Well we could be going someplace around here..."

"We're flying."

"Out of the country?"

"Maybe."

"Oh, come on, David. At least tell me that much."

"Okay," I said. "Yes...it's out of the country."

"Mexico?"

"Are you *serious*, Laci? Do you honestly think I'm going to Mexico any sooner than I have to?"

"I'm sorry," she said softly.

"About what?"

"That you don't want to go to Mexico."

"I'll be fine," I said, kissing the back of her head. "As long as you're there with me I'll be fine."

"I wish you were happy about it."

"I'm happy that we're getting married," I said and she leaned her head back onto my shoulder.

"Me too."

"You know, Laci," I said, "it's really important to me that you understand something..."

"What?" she asked, shifting around so that she could face me.

"You know I'm only going to Mexico because I know it's what God wants us to do..."

She nodded.

"But that's not why I'm marrying you," I said. "I mean, I know God wants us to get married, but I *want* to marry you. I'm not doing it just because God wants me to. Do you understand what I mean?"

She nodded and I could see her smile slightly in the fading light.

"Do you want to marry me?" I asked quietly.

"Of course I do! Why would you even ask me that?"

"Well...because. I know that God told you that you were supposed to marry me..."

"He did, David, but I'm not marrying you because I feel like I *have* to. I love you. I *want* to marry you."

That made me feel very good. She kissed me and that made me feel even better.

"I never even proposed to you," I said.

"You didn't?"

"Uh-uh. We just kind of started talking about it. I mean...I never *officially* asked you."

"Oh."

"Laci?"

"What?"

"Will you marry me?"

In the faint light I could see her smile broadly at me.

"Yes. I'll marry you."

"I love you."

"I love you, too," she said.

"I've got something for you, but you're going to have to move...it's in my pocket."

"David...I thought we decided not to do that."

"No, *you* decided not to do that and then *I* decided that you were wrong. Now *move*."

She moved and I dug the ring out of my pocket.

It was just a single diamond...nothing pretentious. Laci would never go for pretentious.

"It's beautiful," she said as I put it on her finger. "Thank you."

"It's too dark for you to see it," I said. "How do you know?"

"Because, I just know," she laughed. "It's perfect."

"What's so funny?"

"I love it," she said. "I can't believe I actually thought I didn't want one."

"Are you going to show it to all your girlfriends?"

"Of course I am!" she said. "I can't wait!"

I decided that there was a lot to be said for a *typical* engagement.

"Are you still feeling bad?" she asked.

I told her no and then I wrapped my arms around her and held her for a long time.

I'd never felt better.

Six days and one wedding later, I woke up beside Laci. She was still asleep. I started brushing her hair from her face with my fingers until her eyes opened.

"Good morning," I said. "It's time to wake up."

She smiled at me and rubbed her eyes.

"Good morning," she said. "How'd you sleep?"

"I didn't sleep. I just laid awake all night and watched you."

"You did not," she laughed. "What time is it?"

"About eight..."

"What time do we have to be to the airport?"

"We'd better get there by noon," I said.

"Then why do we have to get up?" she asked. The airport was only about ten minutes from our hotel.

"I didn't say it was time to *get* up...I said it was time to *wake* up."

"What are you thinking about?" I asked. We were sitting at the airport, waiting for our flight to be called. She still didn't have any idea where we were going for our honeymoon.

"Just wondering about what kind of surprises are in store for us in our future..."

I looked at her skeptically.

"What?" she asked.

"I don't think there'll be a whole lot of surprises..."

"What do you mean?"

"Nothing," I said, shrugging "just that you're pretty predictable."

"I'm not *predictable*!" she said. "What are you talking about?"

"Laci, are you serious? You're probably the most predictable person I know!"

She stared at me with her mouth open and didn't say anything.

"You don't think you're predictable?"

She shook her head at me.

"You wanna hear how it's gonna go?" I asked.

She nodded.

"Okay," I said. "We're going to fly to...to *somewhere* today, and when we get there you're going to complain about how much money it must be costing and how we could be saving a lot of hungry children or something with all that money instead of 'wasting' it on ourselves. I'll spend the first three days trying to convince you to relax and enjoy yourself and you're going to be so anxious to get to your new job in Mexico that your mind won't even be with me. How'm I doing so far?"

She pursed her lips together because she knew I'd pegged that just about right.

"Then," I continued, "we'll arrive in Mexico and decide on our house. Of course it's got to be a BIG house because you're going to want to have about ten or twenty babies, plus we'll want lots of room for the kids when they come to our house for the outreach program."

She was going to be working for a Christian outreach organization...the same one we'd volunteered with when we'd gone to Mexico on our mission trip the summer before we'd started high school.

"We're going to have Cheerios and lollipops in the carpet and we'll never get to have any good furniture or dishes or anything because all the little rugrats will destroy anything nice."

"Our rugrats or the outreach rugrats?" she asked.

"Both."

"Okay," she said. "Go on."

"I'm right so far, aren't I?" I asked.

She bit her lip and gave me a tiny smile.

"Maybe."

"There's no *maybe* about it," I said. "I'm totally right and you know it."

"Well, keep going," she said. "What else?"

"Okay. Well, let's see. You're going to be taking the youth groups to the orphanage about twice a week, right?"

She nodded. We hadn't done that when we'd gone down there...we'd only ministered to children who had lived in a landfill.

Lived in a landfill.

"All right then. I suspect I'll be getting a lot of calls from you at the orphanage. 'David? Do you think you could come over here and try to fix this door? David? There are some wires sticking out of a wall and I'm afraid one of the kids might get shocked. Would you come and take a look at them? David? They really need me to stay late...would you mind picking up some Chinese take-out?"

"Chinese take-out?"

"Anyway...so then you'll get pregnant and you'll keep working about 80 hours a week until the baby's due and then we'll fly home so we can be with our parents when the baby comes and you and your mom are going to buy him every outfit that's available in Cavendish."

"*Him?*"

"And then," I continued, ignoring her, "we'll fly back to Mexico with the new baby and carry on until you get pregnant again. This cycle will pretty much repeat itself until you hit menopause.

"OH!" I said. "And I almost forgot! In the meantime, you'll keep growing your hair out and sending it to Locks of Love until it turns grey!"

"They take it even if it's grey..." Laci said.

"What little kid wants a wig made out of grey hair?"

"They sell it..."

"Oh," I said. "Okay, so then you'll be doing that until you die. Anyway, admit it. That's pretty much the way it's going to be."

"And what are *you* going to be doing during all this time?" she asked.

"Working like a dog and hoping for a little bit of your time, I guess."

She smiled at me, but then turned serious.

"What if that's exactly what happens?" she asked. "How are you going to feel about it?"

"It doesn't matter how I feel about it," I said. "I'm just along for the ride."

"It does *too* matter how you feel about it," she argued. "I want you to be happy."

"I am happy."

Laci looked at me with concern.

"I don't really want anything," I said, kissing her. "Except to be with you."

"Oh, come on now," she said, smiling. "If you could do *anything*...what would you do?"

"Laci! There's no point in even having this conversation. God wants me to go to Mexico so I'm going to Mexico. I haven't even thought about what I'd do if it was up to me...I really don't know."

"Oh," she said, "I do. I know *exactly* what you'd do. I'm not the only one who's *predictable*!"

"I'm not predictable!"

"Right..."

"What then?" I demanded. "What would I do?"

"Okay," she said. "We'd stay fairly close to Cavendish... but closer to the ski slopes than Cavendish is. We'd probably live on the water somewhere...like a cabin on Cross Lake or something. We'd go water skiing in the summer and snow skiing in the winter and fishing no matter what the weather...how am I doing so far?"

I grinned at her...that actually sounded pretty good. Maybe I was predictable.

"Oh!" she continued. "And our cabin would have a hot tub! I know how much you like a hot tub. As a matter of fact, I may not know where we're going for our honeymoon, but I would almost bet my life that there's going to be a hot tub there. Am I right?"

"In our room," I nodded.

Her mouth dropped open.

"You're kidding!"

"No, I'm not."

She shook her head and I knew she was trying not to ask me how much all this was going to cost.

"I know this isn't exactly your first choice of things to do..." she said.

That was an understatement.

"And," she continued, "I just want to do whatever I can to make you happy."

"You already do," I said, rubbing her hand.

"That's sweet," she said, "but I'm serious. You've got to let me know what you want."

"There *are* a couple of things that I want..." I admitted, looking down at our hands and touching her rings.

She tucked a leg underneath her.

"Tell me," she said.

"Three actually," I finally said. "Three things that I really want and then you can have your way about everything else."

"What are they?"

The first two were easy and I didn't think she'd give me a hard time about them so that's where I started.

"First of all," I said, "I want you to promise me that you'll forget about everything else and just enjoy our honeymoon. Don't think about going to Mexico...don't think about how much *money* it's costing. Just relax and let's enjoy being there and being with each other. We're never going to have this time in our lives together again and it would be really nice if we could try to make the most of it."

"I promise," she said, "but I'd enjoy it even more if I knew where we're going."

I hadn't even let her look at her boarding pass when we'd gone through security and I'd made her sit with her back to the gate where the flight was posted.

"You're going to know soon," I said, looking at my watch. "As a matter of fact, if you listen carefully you're probably going to hear an announcement for our flight pretty quick."

We were going to France. As soon as we'd gotten back from our mission trip and started high school, Laci had switched her elective language class from French to Spanish because she knew she'd be going back to Mexico one day. The French class (the one she'd dropped out of) had gone to Paris when they were juniors. Laci had never complained about it or anything – she'd never even mentioned she was aware that they were going or that she was missing it. But *I* knew she'd missed it and I wanted her to go now.

"What are the other two things?" she asked.

"Whatever house we get, I'm going to need an office."

She nodded. I was fortunate enough to have found a job with an engineering firm that allowed me to work from my home...even a home in Mexico. My degree was in structural engineering with an emphasis in earthquake engineering. In addition to working with architects to design buildings, I'd be doing a lot of international work – traveling to areas after an earthquake to inspect buildings for structural damage. As long as I had the Internet I could really work from anywhere and Mexico City wasn't actually a bad place to be based out of.

“I need my office to be completely off limits to kids,” I said. “ALL kids. Our kids, the outreach kids...I can’t have juice down in my keyboard and grilled cheese sandwiches smeared all over my scanner.”

She smiled at me.

“I mean it, Laci. I need a space to myself...you know? Something that’s just mine.”

“Are you going to let *me* come in?”

“Yeah, right,” I said. “Like you’re going to have any time for me...”

“David,” she said, cocking her head at me. “Come on...”

“So,” I said, smiling, “that’s the second thing, okay? No kids in my office. Not even *one*...not ever! Got it?”

“Got it,” she said. “What’s the third thing?”

I hesitated because I wasn’t sure how she was going to react. I also wasn’t sure why I felt so strongly the way I did. I didn’t know if God was leading me or if I was just trying make myself feel better about my lousy attitude toward Mexico.

“I want you to talk to Aaron when we get to Mexico,” I said. Aaron had been our program leader when we were on our mission trip and now he was the director of the entire Mexico City outreach program. He’d hired Laci.

“About what?” she asked.

“I want you to tell him that you won’t accept a salary.”

“*What?* What do you mean?”

“I mean...you can do the same job he hired you for and you can work as long and as hard as you want to...but I don’t want you to take a paycheck.”

“*Why not*?”

“I want to support what you’re doing...I guess it’s my way of trying to help out. Aaron can use the money to hire another staff member.”

“There’re lots of ways you’re going to be able to help out, David”

“I don’t want to, Laci,” I said, shaking my head. “I don’t want to go back to that landfill...I don’t want to get to know these kids...I really don’t want to be involved.”

She tilted her head at me.

"Do you really think that you're going to be able to live down there and have all those kids in our house and not get *involved?*"

"Probably not...but I can try."

She gave me a slight smile.

"Anyway," I said. "I just feel really strongly about this... that this is how I want to help out right now. Are you going to be okay with that?"

"I think it's fantastic," she said, her smile growing.

"Really?"

"Really," she nodded.

"*Your attention please...Flight 1873 to Paris will begin boarding in five minutes. Flight 1873 to Paris will begin boarding in five minutes.*"

"Is that ours?" she asked.

I grinned at her and nodded.

"*Paris*?"

"You don't want to go to Paris?"

"Isn't that going to be really expen–" she caught herself just in time.

"Come on now, Laci. I'm only asking for three things here and then you can have your way about everything else. Enjoy our honeymoon, keep the little rugrats out of my office, and let me support you. I'll never make you do anything else. Do we have a deal?"

"Deal!" she said, kissing me and wrapping her arms around me.

I hugged her back and I really did mean what I was saying.

I had no idea that one day would I would force her to leave Mexico even though she desperately wanted to stay.

After a week in France we arrived in Mexico and decided on a house within two days (the *pink* one). My accountant (Dad) had convinced me not to rent, but to buy something right away. Even though it could be hard for foreigners to legally purchase property in Mexico, they could do it easily by having a bank hold it in trust for them. Dad had assured me that I couldn't go wrong.

The pink house was vacant and they agreed to let us rent until we were able to close on it, so we were able to move in right away. It had lots of rooms and no lawn...just a courtyard with gravel and weeds.

Laci designated the biggest "extra" room as my office and I spent my first few days there setting it up. My mom had gotten pictures from the mothers of my best friends and had them blown up large. I'd asked mostly for pictures that included us in the snow, but there were some others too, like the ones taken at the pool and one from Cross Lake in the summer. She'd sent them along pressed in thick cardboard sleeves and I had them all framed.

There were five by sevens of our high school senior pictures – me and Laci, Greg, Tanner and Mike – and I had those all matted and put in one frame together.

My favorite one was of me and Greg and Greg's little sister, Charlotte. Charlotte was buried up to her neck in the sand and Greg and I were sitting on either side of her, the surf pounding the shores of the Gulf of Mexico in the background. I also liked the one of the six of us gathered around a snowman in Greg's front yard.

I bought a nice adjustable desk chair and hung the leather jacket that Greg had given me over the back of it and I upgraded the speakers that the company provided with my computer so that I could listen to all my music.

One afternoon Laci poked her head into my office.

"I got you these," she said, handing me some CDs.

"What are they?" I asked, looking them over.

"Just listen to them while you're working and they'll help you learn Spanish," she explained.

"I don't think so," I said, handing them back to her.

"Why not?" she asked, looking hurt.

"I've got some Spanish CDs already," I said.

"You do?"

Now she looked pleasantly surprised.

"Uh-huh," I said, flipping through my collection. "Here's Jaci Valesquez...and I've got Salvador in here somewhere too."

"That doesn't count," she said, putting her hand on her hip. "They're all from Texas."

"They are?"

She nodded and raised an eyebrow at me.

"Well," I said, "they're Hispanic and they make Spanish CDs..."

"And do you *have* their Spanish CDs or do you just have their *English* CDs?"

She knew the answer so I didn't respond. I just smiled at her.

"David!" she said, waving the CDs at me. "You *have* to learn Spanish!"

"Why?"

"Because!" she said. "You're going to live here for...for..."

"*Forever*?"

"No...you're going to live here until..."

"*Until I die*?"

She glared at me.

"You *have* to learn Spanish, David!"

"I can't..."

"Of course you can!"

"No, I can't," I argued. "I've already got two languages in my head...there's no room for any more."

"You don't have *two* languages in your head," she scoffed. "You barely have *one* language in your head."

"How do you calculate the nominal shear strength of reinforced concrete-encased steel panel zones in beam-to-column connections?"

"*What*?"

"Exactly!" I said. "You don't speak my work language, why should I have to speak yours?"

"Because you're LIVING here! If I had to *live* in your computer I'd learn your nerd language too!"

"As if you could..." I laughed.

"I could if I had to."

"Okay," I said. "I'll find some differential equations from one of my *freshman* math classes, and every time you solve one of them correctly I'll learn a new Spanish phrase. How's that sound?"

"You're impossible," she said.

"Let me know when you want your first equation," I replied, grinning at her.

She sighed heavily and walked away.

We'd been in our house for about two weeks and I was sitting at my computer answering an email from a client in Los Angeles when Laci bounded into my office. It was our anniversary – we had been married for a month.

One month.

"I'm pregnant!" she said.

"Yeah, right." I replied. I didn't even look up from my computer.

"David!"

"What?"

She grabbed my shoulder and spun me around in my chair until I was facing her.

"I'm *pregnant*!"

She had about the broadest smile on her face that I had ever seen.

"No, your not," I said, shaking my head and trying to figure out if that was even possible.

"Do you want to see the little test stick?"

"Laci!? How could you possibly be pregnant? What'd ya do? Get pregnant on our *honeymoon*?"

"Apparently!" she said, grinning.

"I want a divorce..."

"Oh, stop it!" she said, hitting me on the shoulder. She sat on my lap and gave me a big hug.

"You're really serious?"

She nodded and then began to look worried.

"You're not mad, are you? I mean...you said I could have all the babies I wanted."

"I know, but I kind of thought we'd warm up with a puppy or something first..."

"You're not mad, are you?" she asked again. She looked even more worried.

"I...I'm...*shocked*," I admitted.

"But you're not mad?"

I just stared at her.

"David!"

"What?"

"Please tell me you're not mad..."

"I'm not mad," I assured her. "I'm...I'm just surprised!"

"You're surprised?"

I nodded at her.

"Why are you so surprised?" she asked, a big smile returning to her face. "I thought you said I was predictable!"

Laci's first doctor's appointment was quite annoying because I could understand *nothing* that Dr. Santos said. Laci had to translate everything. When he put a little white wand on her stomach and I saw the heart of our baby pulsing on the monitor though, I didn't need to be told what was going on.

I booked seats for us to fly home four weeks before her due date and then to return to Mexico six weeks after the baby was supposed to arrive. With my laptop I'd be able to keep up with work without missing a beat and since Laci was working for free Aaron didn't give her a hard time when she told him she was going to be gone for a couple of months.

I checked the dates with Laci before I confirmed our reservations. The tickets were going to be pretty cheap because I was booking them almost seven months in advance.

"You've only got two tickets on the return flight," Laci said, peering over my shoulder at the computer screen.

"Yeah...I figure we can take turns holding him on the way home."

"*Him?*"

"Uh-huh."

"You need to get *her* her own seat," she said.

"Laci!" I said. "Are you crazy? Do you know how much a one-way ticket is going to be?"

"She needs to have her own seat so she can be in a car seat."

"A car seat? Why on earth does he need a car seat on a plane?" I asked.

"It's called *safety*, David."

"There's nothing *safe* about a car seat on an airplane," I argued. "Most people who die in plane wrecks die from the fire after the wreck...not from the wreck itself. Think how much easier it'll be to get him away from the burning fuselage if one of us is already holding him!"

She glared at me.

"Get her her own seat, David," she said.

"You always get your way," I mumbled, adding another ticket to our order.

"Of course I do," she grinned. "We have a deal, remember?"

"I remember," I muttered. "And just in case I don't, you're never going to let me forget."

In the meantime, Laci became engrossed in her work. Anywhere between one to three groups would fly in from the United States or Canada every Sunday. Laci was always in charge of leading one of the groups. She would spend all afternoon training the kids: teaching them a little program of Spanish songs, helping them practice reading Spanish children's books aloud, and telling them their routine for the week.

Her group stayed at a church not too far from the orphanage – rolling out their sleeping bags on the floors of the Sunday school rooms. It was the same church that we'd helped fix up when we'd been on our own mission trip eight years ago.

Sunday night they'd go to the orphanage and learn how to serve dinner to the kids, clean up the dishes, and help get them ready for bed. That's something they would do every night for the rest of the week.

On Monday, they'd come to our house. The same old bus that had picked them up at the airport would arrive, packed full of kids from the landfill. The youth group kids would play with them, read to them, sing with them, and feed them two meals. They would also put on the little program that Laci had taught them.

On Tuesday they would spend the whole day at the orphanage: cooking, reading, playing, singing and changing diapers.

On Wednesday, the youth group kids would take the bus to the landfill and minister to the people who lived there. Thursday, Friday and Saturday were a repeat of Monday, Tuesday and Wednesday. On Sunday the whole thing started all over again when the old youth group flew out and a new one flew in.

Long and short of it, if I wanted to have dinner with Laci, I had it at the orphanage.

I was pleased when I went to the orphanage for the first time to find that it was *nothing* like the landfill. It was clean, it was neat, and the kids were happy and well-fed. The food wasn't too bad either (which was a good thing since I wound up eating there every night of the week).

Usually I kept myself busy after dinner supervising the youth group kids who were cleaning up in the kitchen and then I'd go sit in the back of the common area and watch the program that they put on for the kids. After that, the orphans were bathed and dressed for bed, read to and tucked in.

And that's when Laci would finally let me take her home.

One evening I was sitting in the back of the room, absently listening to the program of songs (which I was already pretty much getting sick of), when a little boy crawled up to me and climbed onto my lap.

Now I'd never really spent a lot of time around little kids before except for Charlotte, my best friend Greg's little sister. She was just a toddler when I was twelve and they'd moved to town.

This kid was about the same size Charlotte had been when I'd met her, so I figured he must be about a year and a half old. He pressed his shoulder up against me and laid his head against my chest. Then he didn't move.

As a matter of fact, he was so still that I thought he'd fallen asleep. I didn't want to wake him, so I leaned my head very slowly forward so that I could see if his eyes were closed.

They weren't.

He spotted me looking at him and turned his face toward me and smiled. I smiled back. Then he put his head against my chest again and didn't move.

As the kids were singing their last song Laci wandered to the back of the room where I was and sat down next to me. She had an amused look on her face.

"Is he asleep?" I whispered.

"No," she smiled.

So I looked at him again and he smiled up at me again.

"What's up?" she asked.

"I don't know," I said. "He just crawled into my lap."

She looked at him and spoke.

"*Hola chiquito. ¿Que haces? ¿Te gusta Dave?*"

He nodded at her.

"*Me gusta también*," Laci said.

"What's his name?" I asked her.

"I'm not sure," she said. "He just came in the other day, but it's time for him to go to bed. Why don't you go change his diaper and I'll find out which crib is his."

"Change his diaper?"

"Yeah. Change his diaper."

"I don't know how to change his diaper."

"Well, then, you'd better start practicing," she said, patting her tummy. "You need to get good at it..."

"I don't think I should have to start now," I said.

"Come on," she said. "It'll be fun."

"*Fun?*"

"Come on."

I picked him up and carried him over to one of the changing tables that was against the wall. I handed him over to Laci.

"You do it," she said, trying to hand him back. "You've got to learn sometime."

"I'll watch this time," I said. "But I'll do it next time, I *promise*."

"Uh-huh. You've got to put these little pictures in the front," she said, handing me a clean diaper. It had pictures of Elmo all over the strip on the front. I watched as she took off his old diaper and put on a new one. The old one was only wet and not *too* disgusting. She also took off his shirt and then handed him back to me while she went to look for Inez.

"Do you like Elmo?" I asked him. He smiled at me.

"I always liked Elmo," I went on. "And the Count. The Count was my favorite."

He smiled at me some more.

"You don't understand a thing I'm saying to you, do you?"

He had a nice smile though. And black eyes. Not dark brown. *Black.*

"What's your name?"

No response.

Maybe he was too young to talk.

"I'm David," I said, jabbing my chest with my thumb.

He touched my hand.

"Can you say David?"

"Day."

"Hey! You can talk. I'm David. Say David."

"Day."

"Try this," I said. "Dave."

"Day."

"No. Dave...*Dave*."

"Day-Day."

"Daaave...Daaave"

"Day-Day."

"Good enough," I said as Laci walked up to us.

"This is Doroteo," she said. "Doroteo, this is David."

"Day-Day," he said.

"We've already met," I explained.

"His crib's the one over there with the Barney bedspread."

"He likes The Count from *Sesame Street* better," I told her.

I wasn't the only adult sitting at the back while the evening programs went on (there were almost always some chaperones too), but the next night that same little boy made a beeline for me and crawled into my lap. He pressed his head against me again and didn't move.

I peeked into his face and those black eyes stared right back at me.

"Man, your eyes are black," I said. I couldn't even see his pupils. I was sitting with my back to the window and it was still light outside so I put my hand in front of his face and moved it back and forth, trying to see his pupils contract and dilate in reaction to the light.

"What in the *world* are you doing?" Laci asked when she wandered by.

"Seeing if he has pupils..."

"You're so weird."

"Well I'm serious, Laci! What if he was in a car accident or something and they needed to know if his pupils were responsive? How would they tell?"

"I don't think he's going to get in a car accident."

"Well," I said. "You know what I mean."

"I'm sure he has *pupils...*"

"Go get a flashlight!"

"Quit trying to get out of changing his diaper," she said, rolling her eyes at me and walking away.

"What's my name?" I asked him while I was changing his diaper. He just grinned at me.

"You sure are happy, aren't you? Do you remember my name? I'm Dave."

"Day-Day."

"Sure, okay. Let's go find your crib. Where's you're crib? Where's your crib?"

He actually pointed at his crib.

"Do you understand English?" I asked him.

"Day-Day," he said, smiling at me.

"That's right," I said, putting him in his crib. "I'm Day-Day. You're a good boy."

Laci came over as I was pulling his Barney bedspread up to his chin. She yanked the covers right back down.

"What are you doing?" I asked.

"Making sure you put his diaper on right."

"Laci," I said, "I'm an *engineer*. I think I can handle putting a diaper on."

"It's gotta be tight," she said, undoing it and tightening it up.

"You're supposed to be able to get two fingers in there," I argued.

"That's dog collars, not diapers."

I sighed.

"*Buenas noches, Doroteo*," Laci said, leaning down to kiss him.

"Day-Day!" he said, reaching up toward me.

I leaned over and kissed his forehead. His hair smelled like strawberry shampoo.

"Why's he calling you Daddy?" Laci asked as we walked away.

"He's not calling me Daddy," I explained. "He's trying to say 'Dave'."

"It sounds like Daddy to me," she said. Then she smiled and patted her tummy. "I guess that's okay, though. You're going to have to get use to it."

The third night he sought me out again and I must say that it felt kind of good to be singled out as the "go to" lap. He crawled up there, sat down and put his head against my chest.

Immediately I felt something warm all over my lap.

"Whoa!" I said, snatching him up. There was a big wet spot on my jeans.

I caught Laci's eye and she came over.

"Something's wrong," I said, holding him away from my body like he was radioactive.

"His diaper just leaked," she said. "That's all."

"They *leak*? How do they leak?"

"I don't know...they just leak."

"Well, that's stupid," I said. "Here. Take him."

"Just go put a clean diaper on him."

I laid him down on the table and undid the tape on his diaper. As soon as I opened it I could tell why it had leaked...it was soaked. *Absolutely soaked.*

I flagged Laci over to where I was.

"When's the last time they changed his diaper? It must weigh a ton!"

"It does look like it's been a while," she admitted.

I grabbed a diaper wipe and began cleaning him. He immediately started crying.

"What's wrong?" I asked him, upset. "*What's wrong*?"

Laci grabbed a dry washcloth and started patting him. He quieted down.

"He's got a little diaper rash," she said. "See?"

I looked. Even though his skin was very brown, I could tell that it was covered with angry red blotches.

"Poor little guy," I said. "No wonder he has a diaper rash. Why'd they leave his diaper on him so long without changing him?"

"Well, David, there're a lot of kids here–"

"So they have to sit around in wet diapers all day?"

"No," she said, smearing some white ointment on his skin, "but he hasn't been crying or complaining or anything and probably nobody noticed that he needed changing."

"So he gets *punished* because he's a happy baby?" I asked, fastening a clean diaper onto him. "That's not right. Where's Inez? I'm going to talk to Inez."

Laci looked horrified.

"No, David! Inez is doing the best she can...we *all* are and these kids are well cared for. This was just an isolated incident."

"I'm sorry I hurt you," I whispered to him, leaning toward his face. He smiled at me as if all was forgiven.

"I'm going to go see if anybody needs anything," Laci said. "You're not going to talk to Inez, are you?"

"No," I said quietly and Laci left.

"You're going to have to learn to stand up for yourself," I told him softly. "If you aren't happy, you've got to let somebody know...*okay*?"

He nodded at me.

"Do you speak English?" I asked him.

He nodded again.

"Do you speak German too?"

Affirmative.

"Do you own a motor home?"

Another nod.

"You're just extremely agreeable, aren't you?"

Yep.

"I bet I could teach you English though," I said. Then I pointed at myself. "Who am I?"

"Day-Day."

"That's right," I said. "You're a good boy."

After that, the first thing I did when I got to the orphanage was to find him and change his diaper whether he needed it or not. I figured that by the time our baby arrived in March I'd be well practiced.

And one night I brought a flashlight with me.

He did have pupils.

He liked it a lot when I sang to him. He was almost always smiling and I liked trying to make him laugh. Usually anything that tickled him would do the trick.

What he *really* liked was something that involved both singing and tickling.

I was singing *Itsy Bitsy Spider* to him one evening and as I was making the spider walk up and down his body, I noticed that his lower legs were bowed. I asked Laci about it that evening after we'd turned out the lights to go to sleep.

"Don't you think Dorito's legs are kind of bowed out?"

"Who?"

"Dorito."

"You mean *Doroteo*?"

"Yeah."

"I hadn't notice," she said.

"They look kind of bowed out to me," I said.

"Hang on." She turned on the light on her side of the bed and went over to her dresser and looked at the pile of baby books that we'd already accumulated. She came back with two of them and handed one to me. I turned on my light too.

We both looked up bowed legs and were assured that some bowing was normal and was nothing to worry about. The legs usually straighten themselves out without any problem. We turned out the lights and went to sleep.

"How old are you?" I asked him one evening. "Are you one?"

He nodded.

"Are you ten?"

He nodded again.

"Uh-huh."

I carried him over to Inez.

"How old is he?" I asked her.

"We don't really know, Señor David" Inez replied. "He was just abandoned in the park a few weeks ago. I'm guessing about eighteen months, but I'm not sure."

"Oh," I said, walking away with him.

"Who would do that?" I whispered to him. "Who would just *leave* you in a park?"

"Day-Day," he smiled at me, grabbing my ear.

"No," I said. "Day-Day would not do that. Day-Day would *not* leave you in the park."

When Laci came to bed that night I was reading one of our baby books.

"What're you reading about?" she asked.

"Seeing when babies are supposed to start walking."

"It's going to be a while," she laughed.

"Oh," I said. "Not our baby. Dorito."

"You mean *Doroteo*?"

"Yeah."

"What's it say?"

"Most kids should be walking by the time they're eighteen months old. Inez says she thinks that's about how old he is. Don't you think that's how old he is?"

"I don't have any idea."

"Did you know that he was abandoned in the park?" I asked her.

"No."

"How could you have a kid for eighteen months and then just *leave* him in a park?"

"There're a quarter of a million abandoned kids in this city, David," Laci said. "You know that."

"I'd never leave our baby in a park."

"What if that's what was best for him? What if you couldn't take care of him?"

"*Him?*"

"Her. I just said '*him*' because we're talking about Doroteo. Our baby's a girl. What if you couldn't take care of her? Wouldn't you be willing to give her up if that's what was best for her?"

I couldn't even imagine myself in a situation like that.

"It makes me mad," I said, ignoring her question.

"I know," she said quietly. "That's why we're here."

Like I said, the food at the orphanage was pretty good and I actually enjoyed the time I spent there, but after the first month I convinced Laci that we *had* to have some time to ourselves. She finally relented and we started going out to eat together every Friday night. By the end of the week the youth group kids were familiar enough with the evening routine at the orphanage that Laci was almost convinced they could manage without her.

On our first night out we were directed to a booth. I let Laci sit down first and then I started to sit across from her. She caught my hand.

"Sit next to me," she said. "Please?"

I looked at her for a moment.

"Odds or evens?" I asked.

She grinned at me.

"Evens."

"One, two, three."

Laci threw out four fingers as I threw out three. She sighed and I sat down across from her. We hadn't done that since we'd dated in high school. She'd always wanted to sit next to me, but I'd wanted to sit across from her. Greg had said that he didn't blame Laci – that looking at me all through dinner probably made her lose her appetite.

"I hope the program goes good tonight," Laci said, reaching across the table for my hand.

"They'll be fine without you for *one* night, Laci," I said, squeezing her hand. "Why don't you try to not think about work for a few hours?"

Yeah, right.

"I think they should do okay," she went on. "They did pretty good last night, don't you think?"

"I guess," I said, shrugging.

"Don't you think they did good?"

"I don't know. Sure. It's just the same ol' stuff every night..."

I had no idea that I was about to get my first taste of pregnancy hormones in action.

"You don't like the programs?" she asked.

"They're fine, I guess. It just kinda gets boring after a while."

It was a good thing that I was sitting *across* from her because if I'd been sitting *beside* her I may not have noticed that her eyes were filling up with tears.

"What's wrong?" I asked, looking at her, shocked.

"You think it's *boring*?"

"Laci...quit crying. This is nothing to cry about."

"You think it's boring!"

"Well so what! Who cares what I think. I'm not a little kid. They probably need repetition or something."

"No," she said, starting to cry harder. "You're right...it's boring. It's just the same thing week after week. It's *awful*!"

I got out of my seat and slipped in next to her, putting my arm around her shoulder. The waiter came by with our menus. He took one look at Laci, set the menus quietly on the table and went away.

"It's not awful, Laci. You're overreacting."

I didn't know it at the time, but this is *not* the thing to say to a pregnant woman.

"*I'm not overacting!*" she cried. "I'm doing a *terrible* job. I bet the only reason Aaron hasn't fired me yet is because I'm working for *free*!"

"You're not doing a terrible job! You're doing a fantastic job, Laci!"

"I want to do better," she sniffed. "I want to make the programs as good as I can, but I don't have any time to find new stuff to teach them! I can barely get everything done as it is..."

"You don't have to come up with new stuff...let the youth groups do it."

"They don't know Spanish," she argued. "They can't just think up stuff on Sunday and do it the next day!"

"Well they know they're coming down here for *months* in advance. Let them know ahead of time and they can get prepared. All you'd have to do on Sunday night is preview what they've got lined up and make sure it's okay."

"How do I let them know ahead of time?" she asked. She was a lot calmer now (which was good) and I could see she was really thinking about what I'd just said.

"It's called the *Internet*, Laci. You just email them and give them some ideas and stuff. I bet they'll come up with all sorts of good things...songs, plays, puppet shows, games..."

"Email them?"

"Yes. *Email* them. You can send an attachment out with sample ideas and good links for them to go to and stuff. They could bring small instruments with them like harmonicas and flutes and stuff and they could check out books from their libraries...or they could even *make* books to read to the kids and then they could donate them to the orphanage...just give them a bunch of ideas and let them come up with their own stuff."

"What if a group didn't want to come up with their own stuff?"

"Well, then you just put a statement in your email saying that this is *optional* and that you'll train them on Sunday if they don't want to prepare anything in advance."

She was looking happy now.

"Do you think any of them would do it?"

"I bet almost all of 'em would."

"Really?"

"Sure, Laci. Remember when we were in youth group? Imagine if Mr. White had told us we had three months to come up with some program ideas to bring down here with us. What would we have done?"

"We would have had a blast!" she said, smiling.

"Well, *you* would have," I said, rolling my eyes. "And then you would've had the rest of us spending three months making sock puppets or something."

"Can you imagine what Greg would have come up with?" she asked, laughing.

"I don't think I want to," I smiled. "The point is, everyone'll come up with something different...and each week'd be something new. I bet you'd get some great stuff. Just make up some real specific guidelines...like make sure they understand that they need to communicate the message of Jesus Christ to these kids and that it needs to be appropriate for all ages, and that it needs to be *fun*. It'll kind of be like they're planning a vacation Bible school or something."

"Will you help me?"

"Help you what?"

"You know...with the emails and the attachments and the links. I don't know how to do any of that stuff."

"You know, Laci," I sighed, "the computer doesn't bite. One of these days you're going to have to join the rest of us in the twenty-first century."

"*Nos reuniremos en el siglo veintiuno tan pronto aprendes hablar español.*"

"Very funny, Laci."

"You don't even have a clue what I said."

"I know enough to know that it was some smart-mouthed remark..."

"Are you going to help me?"

"Are you going to start crying again if I say no?"

"Probably."

"Then I'll help you," I said, trying not to smile as she wrapped her arms around me and hugged me.

Sitting beside her wasn't so bad.

It took me about a week to get a good email together, but I was able to send it out by the middle of July. By the time I was done I had no doubt that we were going to see some awesome stuff from the youth groups that received it. I got the email list from Aaron and sent it to everyone who would be arriving anytime between the middle of August and the following July.

The first group was going to have over a month to get ready and I was really looking forward to seeing what they would come up with, but two days before they were scheduled to arrive there was an earthquake near Los Angeles and I had to fly out just before they flew in.

It was my first site visit and really I was just there to learn – a senior engineer from our company was going to be showing me the ropes. Our job was to go to areas that were minimally affected and verify if the structures needed to be condemned or not.

Laci called me that evening.

"Hi," I said.

"Did I wake you up?"

"Wake me up?"

"Yeah. Isn't it midnight there?"

"No, Laci. It's eight o'clock. I'm two hours *behind* you."

"Oh, yeah," she said. "Is the damage bad? I've hardly seen anything on the news about it."

"No," I said. "It's not bad at all and we're right at the epicenter. I mean...there'll definitely be some insurance claims and everything, but it's not bad."

"Oh, good," she said. "Thank you for the teddy bear."

I'd nestled it between our pillows under the bedspread.

"It's not for you," I said. "It's for the baby."

"Well, I'm going to sleep with it until you get back."

"Okay."

"Guess what?!"

"What?"

"The group from North Dakota's here!"

"I know. Did they have anything prepared?"

"You wouldn't believe it, David! You just wouldn't believe it! They've come up with the greatest stuff! I can't wait until they show it to the kids tomorrow..."

"That's great, Laci. I miss you."

"I miss you too," she said, barely pausing to breathe. "They've got this portable karaoke machine and they're going to let the kids come up and sing into the microphone and then they're going to record it and play it back for them."

"I love you, Laci."

"I love you, too. And guess what? They brought a video camera and they're going to videotape the kids and then they're going to project it onto the wall so that they can see themselves singing and dancing. Don't you think they're going to love it?"

"I'm sure they will."

"Doroteo was asking for you tonight," she said.

"Really?"

"Yep. He kept saying: '*¿Donde esta Day-Day? ¿Donde esta Day-Day?*' over and over."

I didn't say anything and I could practically *hear* her rolling her eyes at me.

"It means 'Where's Day-Day?'," she explained.

"I know what it means."

"Liar," she said. "Anyway, I can tell he really misses you."

"Well," I said. "Tell him I'll be back in about three days..."

"Okay."

"David?"

"What?"

"I really do love you," she said. "And I really, *really* do miss you."

"I love you, too," I said, smiling.

"I hate being alone."

"You're not alone," I said. "At least you've got the baby. I'm the one who's alone..."

"How often are you going to have to go out of town like this?" she asked.

"I guess it all depends on how many earthquakes there are."

"I *hate* earthquakes," she sighed.

"Me too."

"I mean I really, *really* hate them. This teddy bear's not gonna to cut it."

"I know."

"I love you."

"I love you too."

I got back just in time to see what the North Dakota youth group had come up with. The kids definitely enjoyed it, but the best part was that a weight seemed to have been lifted from Laci. She was three months pregnant now and finally admitting that she was feeling a whole lot more tired than she'd expected.

My first night back at the orphanage, Dorito *turbo* crawled over to me as soon as he saw me come in the door. I squatted down next to him.

"Hi!" I said.

"Day-Day!" he smiled. Then he reached his hand up on my knee and pulled himself up.

"Well, look what you can do!" I said, smiling back. I let him wrap his hands around my fingers and I tried to get him to take a few steps because I was thinking that it was about time for him to learn how to walk. That's when I really noticed how bowed his legs were. They were absolutely *not* right. I don't know what it was, but something about seeing him standing on them at that moment made it completely obvious.

Not only did I abruptly realize that his legs weren't normal, but it actually looked so painful that I suddenly couldn't *stand* seeing him trying to walk on those legs.

I scooped him up and carried him over to the changing table, singing to him the whole way.

"What are you looking at?" Laci asked that evening.

The computer screen was full of photos of toddlers with bowed legs.

"I was just trying to figure out what's wrong with Dorito," I said.

"You mean *Doroteo*?" Laci asked.

"Whatever..."

"What'd you find?"

"I think he has Blount's Disease," I said.

"What's Blount's Disease?" Laci asked, looking concerned.

"It affects the upper portion of the tibia and it gets worse as they grow older if it's not treated..."

"But it *can* be treated?"

"Yeah," I said. "If it's discovered early enough they can use leg braces but if it keeps getting worse they have to do surgery..."

"Oh..."

"I think he needs to go see a doctor."

"You know they don't have the money for something like that..."

"We'll pay for it."

"We can't do that..." Laci said.

"Why not?"

"David," she sighed, shaking her head. "Every day I see kids that I want to do more for...kids that I want to give something extra to or really help in some other way, but I can't. You aren't going to be able to get involved with every kid you come across that needs your help...you just *can't*."

"I won't," I promised. "Just Dorito."

"*Doroteo...*"

"Whatever."

I made arrangements with Inez to let me take Dorito to the doctor. Laci went with me so that she could translate. They took x-rays and ran all kinds of tests on him and he was a little trooper, only crying when they pricked his finger to draw blood.

"Don't cry, Dorito," I told him. "They're going to help make your legs work better."

"He doesn't understand anything you're saying because you refuse to learn Spanish," Laci said.

"He will. If I only speak English to him he'll learn it and then he'll be bilingual...that'll really be an advantage to him when he's older."

"Yeah," Laci scoffed. "*That's* why you're doing it."

"What do you think, Dorito?" I asked him. "Don't you want to learn English?"

He nodded.

"And you've got to stop calling him Dorito," Laci complained.

"Why?"

"Because," she said. "His name is *Doroteo*. You're going to get him all confused."

"No I'm not. It's a nickname. Lots of kids have nicknames."

"It's not a nickname," Laci said. "It's a chip..."

"Remember that guy that played saxophone in high school? His name was Chip..."

Laci rolled her eyes at me.

"Dorito's a great nickname," I went on.

"You're going to offend someone," she said. "I don't think it's appropriate for you to be calling him Dorito."

The doctor came in. He and Laci babbled back and forth to each other in Spanish. I avoided saying *Dorito* while they talked.

"He doesn't think it's Blount's Disease," Laci said as the doctor pushed Dorito's legs gently up to his chest.

"What's wrong with him then?"

"He thinks it's probably rickets, but he'll have to wait until some of the test results come back."

"Rickets?"

I hadn't looked that one up on the computer yet. Laci nodded.

"Find out more about it," I said.

Laci talked to the doctor some more while I waited impatiently.

"It's usually due to poor nutrition," she said. "He needs to be on supplements...he needs lots of milk with vitamin D...he needs to go out in the sunshine everyday..."

"Will the bowing go away?"

More Spanish...

"He might get better just as his nutrition improves, but he might need orthotics and physical therapy."

"But then he'll be alright?"

Spanish...

"He could be perfectly normal one day..."

"Well," I said, feeling happy. "That's good!"

"Do you know how much physical therapy and orthotics would cost?!"

"See if he can send us to someone who speaks English."

"You're going to pay for all this?"

"Yeah," I said, tickling Dorito's neck and making him giggle. "And I'm going to teach him English too."

The orthotist made casts of Dorito's feet and fitted him with plastic leg braces. He told me to watch for any discoloration of the skin or any signs of pain. I checked him very carefully every day because he was so happy all the time that I figured he'd have a big piece of skin rubbed raw before he'd bother to complain about it.

The bilingual therapist that we were referred to was named Sonya. Dorito loved her. She made everything seem like a game to him and she showed me exercises to do with him on the days that we didn't see her. Mostly it was a matter of encouraging him to put weight on his legs: trying to walk, squatting down, and standing on his tip toes.

"Sonya said Dorito's really doing great," I told Laci as we were walking home one night about three weeks after Sonya had first seen him. It was a twenty minute walk from the orphanage to our house and we usually only drove if it was rainy.

"David! You've *got* to stop calling him Dorito! You say you want to help him and give him all the advantages you can...but you keep calling him *Dorito!* Do you honestly think that's going to be an advantage to him as he gets older? He's going to get teased by all the other kids!"

"Do you know what 'Dorito' means in Spanish?" I asked her.

She looked at me suspiciously and I knew that she didn't.

"It means 'little pieces of gold'. It's a great nickname."

"How'd you know that?" she demanded.

"Internet..."

"Do you know what 'Doroteo' means?" Laci asked him the next evening at dinner. She was looking at him, but the fact that she was speaking in English told me she was holding this conversation solely for my benefit.

He looked at her blankly so she went on.

"It means 'gift from God'," she said, smiling. "Isn't that nice?"

He nodded at her.

"Oh, my," I said. "I see somebody else has been hitting the Internet too..."

Still smiling, she raised an eyebrow at me, but I wasn't about to be outdone.

"Watch this!" I told her. I turned to Dorito.

"What's your name?"

"Dorito!" he told me.

"That means 'little pieces of gold'," I told him. "Isn't that nice, too?"

He smiled and nodded at me and I saw Laci rolling her eyes.

"And do you know what you are?" I asked him.

"A good boy!"

"That's right," I said. "You're a good boy. Who am I?"

“Day-Day!” he said, still smiling.

“That’s right,” I said, pointing at his plate. “Now eat your corn.”

“Corn,” he repeated.

“*Maíz*,” Laci said.

“Corn,” Dorito and I said together.

I was spending a lot of time in medical offices. If I wasn't taking Dorito to the doctor or to the orthotist or to physical therapy then I was taking Laci to the obstetrician. I think her doctor got big bucks every time he did an ultrasound because he wanted to do one just about every time we went, but I didn't complain. Surprisingly, (to me) he had the latest in technology and most of the time when we left his office it was with a disc full of images of our baby. I didn't waste any time loading them onto my computer and streaming them all together.

In early October we drove to Laci's sixteen-week appointment. This one was especially exciting because (according to all the books) we'd be able to find out what the sex of our baby was.

"I hope she's not turned the wrong way," Laci said.

"I'm sure we'll be able to tell he's a boy."

"This is the last time we're going to get to have this argument," she said. "It's kind of sad..."

"We don't have to find out," I reminded her.

"What do you want to do?"

"I wanna find out," I said.

"Me too."

The doctor talked rapidly in Spanish and I could tell from the big, broad smile on Laci's face that she'd been right. I looked at the screen, hoping to see some evidence of a boy, but even I could tell I was looking at a little girl.

It was funny though, because in an instant – just like that – a little girl was exactly what I wanted.

I started picking Dorito up two or three times a week to get him out into the sunshine and to do his exercises with him away from the orphanage. Often we went to the park, but if the landfill kids weren't at our house sometimes I'd take him there.

In my office we'd go to the *Sesame Street* website and I showed him who The Count was. I let him sit on my lap and look at videos of the baby on the computer screen and I taught him how to say "baby".

I pasted little colored shapes on the wall of my office, just barely out of his reach. The point of it wasn't really for him to learn his shapes or his colors in English (although he happened to be picking up on that pretty quick), but to get him to stand up on his tip toes and stretch when he pointed at them.

"I thought you didn't want any kids in your office," Laci said one day when she spotted the shapes.

"I haven't had any kids in my office."

"Uh-huh."

"I haven't," I insisted. "Those are for the baby. I'm just getting things ready for her. She's going to be a geometry wiz like her daddy."

"Uh-huh," Laci said again, smiling as she walked away.

The weather in Mexico City was pretty much the same all the time. If you've never been there you're probably thinking to yourself: *hot*. But, in reality, Mexico City is at such a high altitude that that's not the case at all. It's actually pretty nice. But like I said, it's also pretty much always the same:

High of 77, low of 42.

High of 73, low of 41.

High of 75, low of 46.

You get the picture.

They do have a "rainy" season in the summer, but it isn't really all that rainy. I checked the weather back home in Cavendish almost every day and tried to imagine what it was like. The third Wednesday in October, according to the Internet, it was breezy and clear in Cavendish. I knew from talking to my Dad that the leaves were "really pretty this year". Halloween was two weeks away and I was wondering if kids went trick-or-treating in Mexico like they did in the United States when I heard someone at the door.

My first thought was that it was a delivery man dropping off some documents that I'd been waiting for from a client in New Mexico, but usually they just knocked on the door and left. I was already in the hallway when I heard Laci calling me and I started running because she never came home during the middle of the day...*never*.

"David!" She was crying and I just knew something was wrong with the baby. I'd forgotten all about pregnancy hormones.

I got to her and grabbed her shoulders.

"Is Gabby alright?" I asked. That's what we'd decided to call her.

Laci managed to nod.

"Are you sure? Gabby's okay?"

"Yes," she sobbed.

"What's wrong then?" I asked. In my mind I started running down the list of things that it could be...her mom or dad was sick...one of our friends had been killed in a car accident...

She was crying so hard that she couldn't talk. I led her over to the couch and made her sit down.

"Please tell me what's wrong, Laci," I said. "You're really scaring me..."

"Last night," she finally managed, "the youth group from Texas..."

She hesitated for a moment before continuing.

"They broke into the church office..."

"*And?*"

"And they stole the communion wine and some of them got drunk and they damaged the sanctuary..."

I was still thinking one of them must have gotten killed or something since she was so upset.

"*And?*"

"And we've been kicked out, David! The church won't let them stay there anymore!"

That's it?

I probably shouldn't have said it, but I did.

"*That's it?*"

"David!" she cried. "What are we going to do? They were *my* responsibility and now we've got twenty kids who don't have any place to sleep!"

"No. They were their youth leaders' responsibility, not yours, and they can sleep here."

"You don't understand, David," she said, still crying. "The church didn't just kick this group out...they've kicked *us* out. We can't house kids there ever again!"

"I understand," I said. "They can just sleep here...in the living room."

"Really?" she asked, finally calming down which was what I'd wanted all along. "Are you sure?"

"Yes, I'm sure," I said. "It'll be like a big slumber party every night."

Like a slumber party in one of those horror movies where everybody dies...

“Thank you, David,” she said, hugging me.

“Laci, you can’t let yourself get so upset. It’s not good for you or Gabby.”

“I’m sorry,” she said. “I’ve been kind of...emotional lately.”

No kidding...

“I think maybe it’s hormones...” she went on.

Really?

“Are you feeling better?” I asked, rubbing her back.

“A lot,” she nodded. “Are you sure about this?”

No.

“Yes, I’m sure. But Laci?” I said. “There’s just one thing...”

“What?”

“You’re gonna have to have to keep ‘em outta my office.”

By late afternoon when the bus dropped the kids off from the landfill I’d had the entire day to get mad at them. They gathered in the living room before going to the orphanage and they were already pretty somber (because of where they’d just spent the day), but I really let them have it.

“Laci and I worked at that church when we were your age and now we aren’t welcome back there because of something *you* did,” I said. “I know not all of you were involved, but it’s not okay for you to just look the other way if somebody’s doing something wrong.”

I caught the eye of a blonde-haired kid sitting back in the corner and he smirked at me. I remembered seeing him at the orphanage the last two evenings. It seemed like he was always either goofing off or mouthing off. As soon as I saw that smug look on his face I knew that he’d been involved.

It had probably been his idea.

Not that I was being judgmental or anything.

We went to the orphanage after I'd lectured them and everybody was pretty quiet. I was in the kitchen helping load up the commercial dishwasher when I noticed the smug, blonde kid standing around, doing nothing. I walked up to him.

"See that kid over there?" I asked, pointing to Dorito.

"The one with those stupid things on his legs?"

I decided to let that pass.

"Why don't you go over there and change his diaper?"

He sighed heavily and started to walk away.

"Wait!" I said and he turned back around.

"What?"

"He likes it when someone sings to him..."

"*Sings to him?*"

"Yeah. Why don't you sing to him?"

"What am I supposed to *sing* to him?"

"Didn't you learn any songs before you came down here?"

I could tell by the look on his face that he hadn't.

"Well," I said, "sing to him anyway. He's learning English so sing to him in English. It'll be good for him."

He rolled his eyes and walked away. I made a point of passing by a few minutes later. Dorito was smiling up at him, but the smug kid wasn't singing.

"You did a really good job talking to them tonight," Laci said when we got back from the orphanage.

"I sounded like my father," I moaned, laying down on my back, crossways on the bed.

She laughed.

"That's because you're paternal instincts are starting to kick in," she said as she lay down next to me. She put her head on my shoulder and her hand on my chest. "You're going to be a great father."

"You're going to be a great mother," I said, hugging her. "As long as all those hormones go away..."

"That's the only reason you're letting the kids stay here, isn't it? Because I got so upset?"

"Yup."

"I'm sorry."

"I'm probably going to forget that they're here tonight and I'm going to trip over one of them on my way to the bathroom and break my neck..."

"You could use a chamber pot," she suggested.

"A what?"

"A chamber pot. We used one all the time when my mom and dad took me camping. It's just this little–"

"Stop!" I said. "I got the idea. I don't think I'll need a *chamber pot*. I'll just try not to kill myself when I'm walking through the living room. I might kick that blonde-haired kid in the head though if I get a chance."

"He is a bit of a problem," Laci agreed.

"At least we only have to deal with him for a week. His youth leaders have to deal with him all the time."

"What about his poor parents?"

"It's probably their fault," I said. "I bet Gabby won't ever act like that."

"No," Laci agreed. "She's pretty much going to be perfect."

"Like me."

This was our favorite subject...how perfect Gabby was going to be.

"Aaron was really pleased that we're letting them stay here," Laci said.

"I'll bet he was..."

"OH!" she said, yanking her hand off my chest and putting it on her belly.

"What?!"

"The baby!" she said. "I felt her move!"

"Are you sure?"

"Yeah, I'm sure!"

"What did it feel like?"

"Just like butterflies! Just like the books say!"

I put my hand on her belly, but of course it was too early for me to feel anything. I sat up and put my mouth over her belly.

"Hey, baby!" I said. "Hey Gabby! Whatchya doing in there? Are you going to be perfect? Are you going to be perfect like your daddy?"

"Hey!" Laci said. "I felt it again!"

"She's agreeing with me," I said and I smiled before I lay back down next to Laci. She put her head back on my shoulder and I wrapped my arms around her. After about thirty seconds she started to sit up.

"Did you feel her again?" I asked.

"No," she said. "I want to call my mom and tell her."

"Don't leave," I said, reaching for my phone and handing it to her. "Call your mom if you want to, but please don't leave."

She took my phone, but she didn't open it.

"I'll call her first thing in the morning," Laci said and she put her head back down on my shoulder.

The blonde-haired kid who was a "bit of a problem", it turned out, was named Carter. I know this because his youth leaders were yelling at him a lot the next day while I was in my office trying to work.

"Carter! Take that off the fan!"

"Carter! Don't put that in there!"

"Carter! Get down from there!"

I ventured out into the kitchen to try to scrounge up some lunch and Laci looked really frazzled.

When I got back to my office, guess who I found?

Carter.

"What are you doing in here?" I asked.

"Just looking around."

"You're not supposed to be in here."

"Who's that?" he asked, ignoring me. He was pointing at the picture of me and Laci and Greg at the picnic table at Cross Lake.

"Me and Laci and my best friend, Greg."

"Are those your parents?" he asked, pointing at a picture of them holding me as a toddler.

"Yep."

"How come you've got so many pictures all over your wall?"

"Because," I said. "They're all the people that I love and I miss them."

"Do you miss the snow, too?" he asked.

"Yeah. I miss home."

"So why don't you move back?"

"Because," I said. "God wants me to be here right now."

He rolled his eyes at me and I really wished he would leave.

"Do they all still live back there?" he asked, pointing at the graduation pictures of me and Laci, Greg, Tanner and Mike.

"No. Just Tanner – the one on the far right."

"What's he do?"

"He's teaches P.E."

"Oh," Carter said, looking at the pictures more closely. "So that's you...and that's Laci...where's this guy live?"

"That's Mike. He's finishing up his undergraduate degree."

Please get out of my office.

"What about him?" Carter asked, pointing at the remaining one.

Oh, boy. Here we go.

"That's my best friend, Greg. He died almost five years ago," I said. Whenever this came up, it was usually God's way of providing me with some kind of an opportunity so I plowed ahead.

"He and his dad were killed in a shooting at our high school during our senior year."

Carter *laughed.*

"What are you laughing about?" I asked him.

"Your best friend got killed, but you still moved to Mexico because it's what *God* wanted you to do?"

I nodded at him, astonished at how he was able to make me feel.

"You're an idiot," Carter said.

Then he finally left my office.

The next day, Saturday, was their last full day in Mexico.

I was in the shower when Laci hollered at me that the bus was there to pick everybody up to go to the landfill.

"Bye!" I yelled back.

I was looking forward to at least six hours of having the house to myself and being able to work in quiet. That's why I was so surprised when I came out into the living room in only my towel and found *Carter* there, in the sweatpants and t-shirt that he'd slept in. He was watching TV.

"Whoa!" I said, getting a good grip on my towel. "What're you doing here?"

"I don't feel good," he said. "They said I could stay here."

I looked at the TV. He was watching *Scooby Doo* in Spanish.

"What?" he said. "Don't you ever watch TV when you're sick?"

"You're not sick," I said. "Listen, Carter, I know it's really hard to go to the landfill and see how those people live, but–"

"Oh, please," he said, rolling his eyes. "That's not why I didn't go...I'm *sick*."

"You're not *sick*," I said flipping off the TV, "and you're *not* hanging around here all day. Get dressed. I'm taking you to the landfill."

"You can't make me go," he said.

"Wanna bet?"

"Touch me and I'll sue you," he said.

"You can't *sue* me, Carter. We're in Mexico."

Now social studies had never been my thing, but I was pretty sure that wasn't true. I figured social studies wasn't Carter's thing either though...

He looked at me suspiciously.

"Are you serious?" he asked.

"No, I'm just kidding."

"I knew you were lying," he said. "Don't you know Christians aren't supposed to lie?"

"Yeah," I admitted, "but they're not supposed to get drunk and tear up church sanctuaries either."

"Whoever said I was a Christian?"

"Look, Carter," I sighed as I opened the bedroom door. "You might have fooled Laci and your youth leaders, but you're not fooling me and you are *not* staying here all day. I'll be out in five minutes and you'd better be ready to go."

"Why are you here?" I asked as we pulled out of the driveway.

"Because you didn't believe me that I'm sick, remember?"

"No," I said. "I mean why are you here in *Mexico*?"

"Because my parents wanted to get rid of me for a week."

Imagine that.

"You don't really believe that, do you?"

"Yeah," he said. "I do."

"You don't think maybe they wanted you to experience something that could have a positive impact on your life?"

He shrugged at me.

"You know, Carter, I never got to finish telling you about my friend, Greg."

"I pretty much got the gist of it," he said.

"No, you didn't," I argued. "You don't know anything about it."

"Oh," he said. "Sorry. You probably wanted to share your *testimony* with me, didn't you?"

"Um...well, yeah. As a matter of fact, yeah."

"Let me guess," he said. "Your best friend got killed and it was terrible and the only thing that got you through it was *Jesus*..."

How can someone who tries as hard as I do find myself so unprepared so often?

"Look," I said. "You know how I told you that he was shot?"

"Yep," Carter said, nodding his head and crossing his arms. "Him and his dad."

"Right. Well, anyway, the guy that shot him...he was a young guy...his name was Kyle."

"Suicidal?"

"Well," I said, hesitating. "Yeah."

"I figured," Carter said, nodding. "They usually are. Did he kill himself?"

"No."

"Cops kill him?"

"No. Listen Carter, do you want to hear my version of this or do you just wanna keep talking?"

"Whatever," he said, settling back into his seat.

"Okay. Kyle surrendered and he was sentenced to be executed this past spring."

"Did they do it?"

"Yeah..."

"Cool."

"No, Carter," I said, shaking my head. "It's not cool!"

"Oh...you're one of *those*..."

I was completely exasperated. I had never met anyone like this in my entire life. Witnessing to Kyle had been a snap compared to this.

"Look," I said, talking faster in hopes that he wouldn't be able to squeeze a word in edgewise. "Laci and I and Greg's mom and some other people, we all went and visited with Kyle and we talked to him about Jesus and how much Jesus loved him and how He'd died for each of us and Kyle accepted Christ before he died."

There...at least I'd gotten that out.

"You really believe that?" Carter scoffed.

"I *know* that," I said.

"Whatever."

"Greg always put Christ first in his life," I went on, ignoring him. "God was the most important thing to him. He would have gladly given his life to keep Kyle from dying before he was saved."

"Sounds like he did," Carter said. "Glad it all worked out."

"No," I argued. "He didn't have any choice about it, but what I'm saying is that Greg would have willingly died to keep someone – *even a total stranger* – from dying if they didn't know Christ."

"Would you do that?" Carter asked, a trace of seriousness in his voice for the first time.

"I'd like to think so," I said, "but I hope I never have to find out."

"What about your baby? Or Laci?"

"What do you mean?"

"I mean what if there was a fire or something and you could only rescue one person? Let's say you had to choose between Laci or someone who wasn't saved. Like what if you had to pick between me and Laci?"

Who was *this kid?*

"Well, again, Carter, I hope I never have to find out what I'd do in a situation like that, but I'd like to think that I'd rescue *you*."

"Yeah, right," he laughed.

We were almost to the landfill.

"I'm serious, Carter. You may not believe it, but there's another life after this and it's going to last *forever*. The thought of anybody going through eternity separated from Christ..."

I shook my head and glanced at him.

"I want you to know that Laci and I prayed for you last night."

He didn't say anything.

"We prayed that you'd know Christ...that you'd know what He did for you."

"Thanks," he said as I pulled alongside the parked bus, "but I already know *all* about it."

"We'll keep praying for you," I said. He was reaching for his door handle.

"Don't do me any favors," he replied and he got out and slammed the door.

We always had a "service" for the youth groups in our home on Sunday morning before they were taken to the airport. It was usually a special time and we always invited the kids to come forward and commit their lives to Christ and while we lived in Mexico many of them did.

I'd love to be able to tell you that the next day Carter was one of them...

But he wasn't.

Carter sat through the entire service as if he was bored out of his skull and when it was over he got on the bus and plopped down in his seat and never looked back.

After the group from Texas went home, Laci and I continued to pray for Carter. I'm sorry to say that I don't know whatever became of him. After he left I found myself thinking a lot about the last time that I'd been to the landfill. I'd been about Carter's age.

I'd gone there with Mike and Greg and we'd tried to share Christ with a crippled boy who lived in the landfill. Mike was worried afterwards, complaining that we'd never know if we'd done any good or not.

Greg had assured him that we would...that one day we'd know.

I may not know what became of Carter, but I do believe what Greg said.

I believe that one day I'll know.

There's one thing that I already know right now though.

The last night, while we were at the orphanage, I saw Carter at one of the changing tables. He was putting a clean nightshirt on Dorito after dinner.

I walked over near where they were. I didn't get *too* close, but I got close enough. Dorito was smiling (of course) and as I passed by, I could barely hear Carter.

He was singing to Dorito – very softly – just under his breath.

Since we were going home in February we stayed in Mexico for Christmas. There were two youth groups scheduled to be with us before Christmas, but only for four days each. We'd be all alone for our first Christmas together.

Christmas morning we went into our living room and sat on the floor by the tree. First we opened the presents sent by our families: Laci's mom and dad, my mom and dad, and my sister and her family. Then Laci held a package out to me.

"I thought we weren't going to buy each other anything," I said.

We'd decided that rather than spending a bunch of money on presents for each other we'd buy a video camera to record every moment of Gabby's life instead. (Of course I hadn't stuck to our agreement either.)

"I didn't really buy it," she said, still holding firmly to the package.

"You made it?"

"Ummm...." she hesitated, her face serious. "No. I mean I did buy it, but I bought it...a long time ago."

She let go of the package and I opened it. It was a sweatshirt from my alma mater – State. I kind of wondered why she hadn't gotten one that said *Alumni* on it, but I wasn't about to ask.

"Thanks, Laci," I said after I pulled it over my head. It could have been a little bigger too. "I love it."

She nodded at me, but she was really quiet.

"I've got something else," she finally said. "But I'm not sure if I should give it to you or not, I'm just not sure..."

"What are you talking about?"

She leaned over and touched my sweatshirt.

"I bought this a *long* time ago," she said again.

"I really like it," I told her and she sighed because I just wasn't getting it.

"I bought it right before..."

She stopped and dropped her eyes to the floor. I reached over and tucked her hair behind her ear.

"Before what, Laci?"

"When we were dating," she finally said, looking back up at me with tears in her eyes. "In high school."

Now I got it. Right before Christmas of our senior year. Right before Greg and his dad had been killed. Right before I'd shut her and everyone else out of my life.

"Oh," I said quietly.

"There's something else too."

"Okay..."

"I have something else, but..."

"What?"

"I bought it for Greg..." she said, almost in a whisper, looking back down at the floor. I saw a tear fall onto her lap. "I didn't know what to do with it."

"Oh."

"I'm sorry..."

"It's okay, Laci. Why don't you show it to me?"

"Are you sure?"

"Yeah...I wanna see it."

She pulled a small package out from under the tree and I opened it up.

It was a compass. Not the kind that points you north, but the kind that's used in math. And not a cheap kind with little golf pencils that every kid takes to school either. It was an expensive one...one that an engineer would use.

"I know you already have one," she said, crying harder, "but I didn't know what to do with it."

"I'm glad to have it," I said and I scooted over next to her so that I could hold her. Usually when she cried I tried to do whatever I could to get her to stop, but sometimes it's good to just let it out. Greg had been my best friend, but I think he'd been Laci's too.

After awhile she wiped her eyes and told me she was sorry again.

"He would have loved it," I said. "It would have gone good with the calculator I got him."

"You got him a calculator?" she asked, looking surprised.

"Uh-huh."

"What'd you do with it? Do you still have it?"

"No," I said. "I gave it to Charlotte."

"He got *me* a calculator too..."

"Greg got *you* a *calculator*?"

"Yeah," she said, shaking her head and wiping her eyes again. "You two were such nerds."

"I don't see you complaining about it now." I poked her in the ribs.

"No," she admitted. It was nice not to have to worry about money.

"So when did Greg give you a calculator? I don't remember this at all."

"His mom said he bought it for me for Christmas. She gave it to me after he died."

"Why would Greg get *you* a calculator? Do you think it was a joke or something?"

(Math wasn't Laci's thing.)

"Maybe," she said. "Or maybe it was because the two of you weren't going to be able to help me with math anymore after we went off to college."

"A calculator's not going to help you if you don't know what buttons to push," I teased.

"I managed without you," she said smiling slightly. Then she turned serious. "It was hard though. It was a hard four years...not having either one of you."

"I know," I said. "I'm sorry."

"Did you get me anything that Christmas?" she asked me after a moment.

"No," I admitted.

"How come?"

"Because I hadn't figured out what to get you yet. You're impossible to buy for."

"No, I'm not! I'd love anything that you got for me."

"I know," I said, "but I'd wanted to get you something special and that's hard because you don't *want* anything."

"I don't need anything."

"I think I figured out something this year that you're going to like," I said, grinning at her.

"You got me something? You weren't supposed to get me anything besides the video camera."

"I can take it back..."

"No," she smiled, shaking her head. "What is it?"

"Come on," I said, standing up and giving her both of my hands because it was really getting hard for her to get up these days.

We went into my office and I opened up the closet door. There were a hundred and thirteen presents in there...each one individually wrapped with a name tag on it.

It had taken me *forever* to wrap them all.

"What in the world have you done?" she gasped.

"Look at them," I answered, still smiling. I was feeling pretty proud of myself.

She picked up the first one.

"To Hosea...From Santa."

She picked up two more.

"To Selena...From Santa. To Marco...From Santa." She looked at me with her mouth open. "You got one for *every kid* at the orphanage?"

"I couldn't think of anything you'd want more than to go visit them this afternoon and be able to give each one of them something for Christmas," I said. "Am I right?"

She nodded at me and started crying again and then she flung her arms around me and held me tight.

It took a long time that night at the orphanage to tuck everybody in because there were no students to help us. When I put Dorito into his crib he was clutching his new stuffed Elmo.

"You like Elmo?" I asked him. He nodded and grinned.

"You like The Count better, don't you?"

Affirmative.

"Santa told me he really wanted to get you The Count," I went on, "but for some reason they're very hard to come by. Maybe next year Santa should start looking earlier and try eBay. Whatdya think?"

He blinked at me, still smiling. I leaned down and kissed his forehead.

"Good night, Dorito," I said.

"Night, Day-Day."

"Merry Christmas."

The day after Christmas the middle school youth group from our old church in Cavendish flew to Mexico City to spend their week with us. I didn't usually go to the airport when the bus picked up kids, but Greg's little sister, Charlotte, was going to be there, so I went to the airport with Laci and Aaron. We pretty much knew most of the kids, but none of them like we knew Charlotte. Although she seemed pretty happy to see us, I don't think she was as happy as I was.

When I hugged her I felt like I was touching Cavendish.

The youth group had just finished showing Laci all the stuff they'd prepared when I peeked into the living room and looked for Charlotte. She was sitting next to her best friend, Lydia, giggling.

"Pssst..." I caught her eye and motioned for her to follow me into my office. I sat down in my chair and pulled up another one next to me.

"I'm really glad you're here," I said.

"Me too."

"Looks like you got some good stuff to do with the kids..."

"Yeah," she nodded. "I can't wait to meet them. It's going to be fun."

"It's going to be hard, too," I said. "Especially Wednesday..."

That was the day they'd go to the landfill.

"I know," she said.

No you don't. You don't have a clue. I decided she'd find out soon enough.

"I want to show you something," I told her.

I double-clicked the Gabby icon on the screen. The first footage was from about eight weeks. It wasn't too clear that she was a baby, but you could definitely see her little heart beating in the middle of the screen. I glanced at Charlotte and she seemed impressed.

"That's really cool..."

"Just wait," I said. "It gets better."

I pointed out every significant part of each segment in the video, pausing it, rewinding it and playing it again. We were near the end, at the part where Gabby was sucking her thumb, when Laci walked in.

"I can't believe she's sucking her thumb!" Charlotte exclaimed. "I didn't know they did that."

"Sometimes babies are even born with a little blister on their lip because they suck their thumb so much," Laci told her.

Then Laci looked at me. "I thought kids weren't allowed in your office."

"I've been known to make the occasional exception," I assured Charlotte, smiling at her.

"I'm not a kid," she protested. "I'm almost thirteen!"

"Right, sorry!" Laci said, turning to leave. "Oh, and by the way...Charlotte?"

"Hmmm?"

I was pleased that her eyes were reluctant to leave the image of Gabby on the screen.

"I made arrangements with your youth leader for you to stay here for dinner Wednesday night instead of going to the orphanage...if you want to."

I paused the video so that Charlotte could look away from the screen and smile at Laci.

"Thanks! I'd love to," she said. Laci smiled back at her and left, closing the door behind her. Charlotte looked back at me and grinned.

I know my eyes got wide when I looked at her.

"Wow!" I said.

"What?"

"Nothing." I shook my head at her.

"*What?*"

"Nothing," I said again. "You just...I don't know...you just..."

"Look like Greg when I smile?" she suggested.

"Yeah," I nodded. "I mean...you really, *really* looked like Greg just then."

"I get that a lot."

"I guess I never noticed it before. *Wow*."

"Does it bother you?" she asked rather quietly.

"No," I assured her, waving my hands at the pictures on my walls. "Look around...does it look like I'm trying to forget about Greg?"

"I guess not," she admitted, leaving her chair to look at the picture of us in front of the snowman. "I remember that day..."

"Really?"

"Uh-huh," she said. "I remember that Greg got mad at me because I wanted the snowman somewhere different and you made him move it."

"I was always a lot nicer to you than he was," I said and she laughed. I pointed at the picture of us on the beach in Florida. "Remember that?"

"Not really," she said. "I mean, I know you went to Grandma's with us one summer because I've seen pictures, but I really don't remember it."

That kind of bothered me since it had been such a great time for me.

"Actually, I went with you twice..." I told her.

"Really?"

"Yeah. The last two summers..."

"Oh."

We looked at the beach picture for another moment.

"Do you want to see the rest of Gabby's video?" I finally asked.

"Can we see her sucking her thumb again?" Charlotte asked.

"Sure," I said as we sat back down. "It's one of my favorite parts."

On Wednesday evening I dropped Dorito off at the orphanage after physical therapy and then rushed home. He started crying when he realized I wasn't going to stay for dinner and Inez had to pry him off of my legs. When I got to the house, the rest of the youth group was gone and Charlotte was there, helping Laci dish up take-out food.

"Hi!" I said, hugging them both. Charlotte didn't look too happy.

I knew she'd been at the landfill all day so I didn't ask her what was wrong. She was pretty quiet during dinner too, but after we'd eaten she told us, "I got you something for Christmas."

"You didn't have to do that."

"It's from me and my mom...and a few other people too." She was brightening up a bit.

Charlotte went to her suitcase in the living room and pulled a big package from it. The wrapping paper was wrinkled and ripped in a few spots, but she handed it to us without an apology. I sat in the middle of the couch with Laci and Charlotte on either side.

"Let's see what we've got here," I said, tearing off what was left of the wrapping paper. It was a white box, and in that was an album.

I put the box and the paper on the floor and opened the album to the first page. Laci leaned in to see and so did Charlotte. I could see her out of the corner of my eye, glancing into my face to see my reaction.

There were two baby pictures...one of me and one of Laci...side by side. I'd seen mine often, Laci's a few times.

I turned the pages to find pictures of us as infants and then as toddlers...first day of preschool pictures...an Easter egg hunt on the church lawn.

"Oh!" Laci said, pointing to herself at three. "I remember that dress! I loved that dress!"

"Look at that," I said. There was a photo of our preschool class, posing in front of the school building. Laci and I searched for ourselves.

"There you are," I said, finding her easily. "Before you chopped your hair all off..."

"There's Tanner..." Laci said. "Where are you?"

"He's right here," Charlotte said, pointing to the back row. The preschool teacher had her arm firmly on my shoulder as if she were keeping me from fleeing.

"Where'd you get all these, Charlotte?" I asked, turning the page.

"Everybody..." she said. "When your mom started asking around for pictures for your office my mom and I got the idea to do this album. We just told everybody that while they were at it to give us some too. A lot of these are scans..."

They must have talked to Natalie and Ashlyn's parents too because there were pictures of them when they were little. There was a picture of Natalie and Laci at the bowling alley, celebrating somebody's birthday and one of Ashlyn and Laci wearing sunglasses and posing for the camera. There were pictures of my dad, handing Mike a medal for winning the pinewood derby in Cub Scouts, of Tanner standing next to me and holding up a fish, and of Natalie, Ashlyn and Laci all dressed up to go to a dance.

Not only had she included pictures of the Christmas pageant we'd put on in the fourth grade, but of the program that had been distributed at church too. Next to a picture of a grinning Mike (with both of his front teeth gone), she'd put a gum wrapper.

"Oh!" Laci said. "He *always* chewed that kind... remember?"

I nodded.

"This is unbelievable," I told Charlotte. "I can't believe you did all this."

"A lot of people helped."

She'd done everything chronologically. There were pictures of Laci's volleyball teams and track teams and team shots of me and Tanner and Mike in soccer and basketball and baseball. They ranged all the way from the time we were in pee-wee leagues until we'd been in high school. From the seventh grade on, Greg was in the team sports pictures too.

She had a copy of my Red Cross lifeguard certification next to my first paycheck stub from the pool. She'd also included a take-out menu from *Hunter's Pizza and Subs* and next to that was a penny.

"Did you get that penny off Greg's dresser?" I asked her, smiling. Charlotte nodded and smiled back and I shook my head. Every time I'd eaten there when Greg was working I'd tipped him a penny and he'd kept them all in a jar on his dresser. He said he was saving them up to buy a pack of gum.

Charlotte had even found a piece of notebook paper where Greg and their dad and I had worked out some of our AP physics problems.

We were nearing the end when Charlotte suddenly stuck her hand out and stopped me from turning the page.

"For this next part," she said, "I had all your friends tell their favorite memory of you."

"That was a nice idea, Charlotte," Laci told her.

"This whole thing was a nice idea," I said.

I turned the page and saw Natalie's senior picture on the left hand page and two letters (one to each of us) on the right.

Dear Laci:

My favorite memory with you is that time when there was a meteor shower and I came over to your house and we laid out in your driveway and watched it together until about two in the morning.

I'm so glad for all of the times that we've shared together and I'm so excited for you and David. Can't wait to see you both and meet Gabby. Don't have her before your shower! I'll be there.

Love, Natalie

Under that was her letter to me.

Dear David:

My favorite memory of you is of one Halloween when we were probably in the fourth or fifth grade. You and Tanner and Mike came trick-or-treating at my house just when I was getting ready to take Emma out. You picked up one of the pumpkins on our porch (I think you thought it was mine, but it was Emma's) and you were looking at it when Mike accidentally bumped into you and you dropped it and it smashed all over the porch. Of course Emma was crying and howling and playing it up for all it was worth. My mom came out on the porch to help clean it up and try to calm Emma down and you kept apologizing over and over. My mom told you not to worry about it, but I could tell that you felt really, really bad...you actually looked like you were going to cry. That was the first time I thought that maybe you weren't the heartless idiot I'd always pegged you for.

Love ya! Natalie

I looked at Laci.

"Is there supposed to be a compliment in there somewhere?" I asked.

"I think so," she laughed.

Tanner's was worse.

(Don't read this David...)

Dear Laci:

My favorite memory of you? Hands down...prom night!

Love, Tanner

(I told you not to read this, Dave!)

"He's *real* funny," I said. Laci put her hand over her mouth so I wouldn't see her smile. Then we read the one he'd written to me.

Dave:

Just one? I only get to pick one? Okay then, I pick the time I was trying to teach you to drive my dad's stick shift in the parking lot of the high school. You had a bit of trouble with the clutch...remember?

Anyway, this cop pulls up and taps on the window and then makes you get out of the car – he thought you had to be under the influence or something. So he makes you get out and start walking a line and touching your fingertips to your nose and everything and you were like "Really, officer...I'm not drunk! I'm just a bad driver!" I was laughing so hard. I think he was really disappointed that he couldn't write you a ticket. I know I was.

Can't wait to see you guys! Tanner

I just shook my head. I was going to kill Tanner when I saw him again.

Ashlyn's senior picture and letters were next.

Dear Laci-

My favorite memory of us is when you and Natalie would come over to spend the night and we'd make pizzas and drink Mountain Dew. One night we watched scary movies on TV and we got so freaked out. We heard something on the porch and started screaming and my dad came out of the bedroom yelling at us to keep it down and we were like "There's something on the porch! There's something on the porch!"

We were pretty sure it was an ax murderer or something, but Dad flipped on the light and it was a raccoon. He told us we'd better go to sleep and not wake him up again. We didn't wake him up again, but we were too scared to sleep all night!

Love you! Come home soon!

Ashlyn

Dear David-

I remember when we were in biology class together and Tanner and I were lab partners. We took our fetal pig heart and put it inside your pig when you weren't looking and you thought you'd discovered some great scientific freak of nature or something. You showed it to Mr. Powell and everything and he was like "Umm, David? Does anything look a little strange to you about this second heart?" You started poking around at it for a minute and when you figured out it wasn't attached you just looked right back at me and Tanner and glared at us. I said "Uh-oh," but Tanner told me not to worry about it.

Then at lunch he went to go get some ketchup and he found that little heart nestled in his corn when he got back. The funniest part is that putting it in your pig wasn't Tanner's idea...it was mine!

Love, Ashlyn

"Yeah," I said. "That stupid thing wound up in my notebook the next day."

"That's disgusting!" Charlotte said.

"I got even with him though," I went on. "I put it in his locker."

"Yuck," Charlotte said.

"It's not still getting passed back and forth, is it?" Laci asked. "I'm not going to find it in our bed tonight or anything, am I?"

"No," I said. "He threw it at me in history and missed and it kinda landed on Mrs. Butler's desk..."

"Oh, that's so gross!" Charlotte said.

"Yeah," I admitted. "It was pretty gross."

“Did you guys get in trouble?”

“No, she didn’t see it happen...”

“You two just *left* it there?” Laci asked, clearly appalled.

“Let’s get back to the album!” I said, changing the subject.

The next page was Mike’s. Next to his senior picture (taken the year after we’d graduated because he was a year younger than the rest of us) were the letters he’d written.

Dear David:

My favorite memory of you is actually probably several memories strung together, but I remember you coming over to the house and playing chess with my dad. Whenever you saw an opportunity to beat him, you’d do it...and then you’d rub his face in it every chance you got.

Other people always treated him with kid gloves, but you never acted like he was sick or anything. You always made him feel really normal. I appreciated that, and I know he did too.

Merry Christmas!
Love, Mike

Dear Laci:

My favorite memory of you also involves my dad...and my mom. The week after Dad died I had training camp and I was really worried about leaving my mom alone, but she insisted that I go ahead. That whole first day of practice I was really concerned about her and couldn’t keep my mind on things at all.

When Tanner’s mom dropped me off at my house I ran inside, worried about how I would find her, and the first thing that hit me when I walked in the door was the smell of Pine-Sol. And there you were...in the kitchen with my mom, helping her clean the floor, and both of you were laughing and talking. I still think about that every time I smell Pine-Sol.

Take care of that baby! Can’t wait until spring!
Love, Mike

I was a little nervous before I turned the next page. I knew it should be a 'Greg' page, but I couldn't figure out how it possibly would be.

It was though. His senior picture was there, and there were two letters...one to Laci and one to me.

His mom had written both of them.

Dear Laci:

I'm sure I won't be able to pick the same memory that Greg would have, but one thing I really remember is when you came over to help him cut his hair that first time. He was really excited about that. Of course he was also really happy when you and David got together...he always said the two of you were meant to be. He was right! And he'd be so happy to know about Gabby too...maybe he already does.

Love,
Mrs. White

"I didn't know you helped him cut his hair," I said.

"There're a lot of things you don't know," she grinned.

The last letter was the one Mrs. White had written to me.

Dear David:

Just like with Laci, I'm sure I won't pick the same memory that Greg would have chosen, but I've been thinking back on the times when the two of you were together – which was pretty much all the time!

Greg was always pretty happy, but he seemed especially so after his dad took the two of you fishing out on that charter boat.

Remember? He seemed not only unusually contented, but amused too...I don't know what about. I do know, however, that he was really glad that you were able to go to Florida with us.

Not sure if that brings back any special memories for you or not, but I hope so. Can't wait to see both of you and meet the baby!

All my love,
Mrs. White

"*Does* it bring back some special memory?" Laci asked when she finished reading it.

"Probably for him it would have," I admitted. "I was barfing like a dog the whole time we were out on that boat."

Laci laughed and I didn't say anything else, but I knew there was another reason that Greg had been "unusually contented, but amused too".

It was on that trip that I'd told him I knew I wanted my relationship with Laci to be more than just a friendship. Just that thought had turned me into such a nervous wreck that I'd hardly been able to enjoy my week in Florida at all. Greg was happy because he'd really wanted me and Laci to get together, plus he'd always enjoyed watching me squirm.

The rest of the pages were blank.

"These are for you to put pictures of Gabby," Charlotte explained.

"What about you, Charlotte?" Laci asked. "How come you didn't put down *your* favorite memories?"

"I just wanted it to be about you and your friends," she said.

"You're our friend," I told her.

"You know what I mean," she said, and I did.

"Well, tell us what your favorite memories are," I said. "I wanna know what you remember."

"Well..." she said, putting a finger to her mouth and looking at Laci, "I remember you babysitting me. Whenever I found out you were going to babysit I'd always get so excited.

Mom would let me pick out whatever I wanted for dinner and you would make it for me and we'd get to eat it in front of the TV."

"What'd you pick for dinner?" I asked her.

"Spaghettios," Laci answered for her. "Always Spaghettios."

"And Chips Ahoy cookies for dessert!" Charlotte added.

"I could actually go for some of those right now," Laci mused.

"What about me?" I asked.

"Well," she said. "I told you I remember when you made Greg move that snowman for me..."

"Uh-huh. What else?"

"I remember you playing Go-Fish with me in the basement when there was a thunderstorm outside..."

"What else?"

"Um...I remember you helping Greg and my dad take off my training wheels and I remember that one time you let me put barrettes in your hair..."

"Are you sure that wasn't Greg?" I asked skeptically.

"Positive. You let me paint your fingernails too..."

"Okay," I said. "Never mind. I'm sorry I asked."

The next day before the bus brought the landfill kids to our house again, Charlotte stuck her head in the door of my office to say hello.

"Thanks again for that album, Charlotte," I told her. "It's really fantastic. Laci and I looked through the whole thing again two more times before we went to bed."

Charlotte beamed.

"And if you see Tanner you can tell him I was *deeply* touched by his letters..."

"I see him almost every day...remember?"

"Oh, yeah," I said. "I almost forgot that he teaches you."

"I'll probably have him in high school too. I think he's going to try to get a job there," she said. "He's already helping coach some of their teams..."

“Football?” I guessed.

She nodded. “Baseball in the spring, too.”

“Is there going to be a job opening at the high school?”

“Coach Williams is probably going to retire either this year or next.”

“Well,” I said, “I hope for Tanner’s sake that he gets the job. No offense, but I can’t imagine teaching a bunch of middle schoolers all day.”

“I hope he gets it too,” she nodded. “I want him to be our P.E. teacher in high school.”

“He’s a good teacher, huh?”

“Oh,” she said, shrugging, “he’s fine I guess, but Jordan absolutely *hates* having his brother for a teacher. I want Tanner to get the job just so that Jordan will be completely miserable.”

“What’s your problem with Jordan?”

“I can’t *stand* him...” she said, contempt clouding her face.

“You guys use to play together all the time when you were little.”

“Don’t remind me...”

“What’s so terrible about Jordan?”

“He’s disgusting and mean and I can’t stand being around him.”

Tears started welling up in her eyes.

“Sit down,” I said, motioning for her to sit on the small couch that was along the wall. She did. I wheeled my chair closer to her.

“What’s he done that’s so terrible?” I asked her, suddenly feeling very protective.

“Nothing,” she said, running a hand across her eyes.

“Well, Charlotte...he must have done something or you wouldn’t be so upset just *talking* about him...”

“I just don’t like him,” she said. “I don’t want to have anything to do with him...”

“Well then,” I said. “Just stay away from him...”

She looked down at the floor.

“Can’t you just stay away from him?”

“I guess so,” she said. She nodded slightly but I could tell she was far from convinced. She finally glanced up at me.

"What?" I asked her.

She bit her lip and sighed.

"What?" I asked again.

"If I tell you something," she began, "do you promise not to ever tell anyone...*ever*?"

I nodded, but I was thinking that if Jordan had somehow done anything to hurt her that I was going to break that promise very quickly.

She sighed deeply.

"Does God ever tell you stuff?" she asked.

"Sure," I said.

"Like he talks to you?"

"Well," I admitted, "He doesn't really *talk* to me...he leads me, guides me. He talks to me through Scripture though...stuff like that. You know what I mean?"

She nodded.

"That's what he usually does to me too," she said, "but..."

She hesitated for a long moment before going on.

"He told me something," she said. "It was different than just Him leading me or guiding me. It was really *clear*. It wasn't a voice exactly...I can't explain it really. Somehow I just knew it was God...does that make any sense?"

"Sure it does," I said. "Laci's had that happen."

"*She has*?"

"Uh-huh."

"Okay," she said, looking immensely relieved. "Well, God told me..."

"What?"

"Promise you won't tell anyone?" she asked me again.

"I promise, Charlotte."

"Except maybe Laci," she decided. "You can tell Laci if you want to."

"I can't tell her anything if you don't ever tell me..."

She sighed heavily and shook her head.

"What'd He tell you?"

"That Jordan...that Jordan and I..."

She didn't say anything else, but I got it.

"Really?!" I asked, trying very, *very* hard not to smile.

"It's not funny!" she said, on the verge of tears again.

"I never said it was funny," I told her. "I think it's sweet."

"It's not sweet either!" she argued. "I can't stand Jordan!"

"You're talking about something that's years away, Charlotte. You might feel differently about it when you're an adult."

"I doubt it," she said, wiping her eyes again.

"Charlotte, you've got to be faithful to what God tells you."

"I don't want to," she said, shaking her head.

"I know, Charlotte, but..." I paused for a minute. "Can I tell you something?"

"What?"

"God told Laci that she was going to be with me."

"Really?" she asked doubtfully.

"Really," I nodded. "And after Greg and your dad were killed I just pushed her and everyone else away. Did you know that we didn't date the whole time we were in college until last spring?"

"I guess so."

"How do you think Laci felt during that whole time?" I asked her.

She shrugged.

"Don't you think she probably felt like God had made a mistake? Like she didn't want to believe what God had told her?"

Charlotte nodded.

"She probably felt just like you do right now, but she listened to what God said..."

"Did you always like Laci?"

"Charlotte," I laughed, "if you'd told me I was going to marry Laci when I was your age I would have told you that you were crazy. Absolutely *crazy!*"

She gave me a slight smile.

"Please don't get so worried about it right now," I told her. "Just try to enjoy things. One day you're going to be looking through a scrapbook and you'll remember how great these times were. Try to enjoy them while they're happening."

"Did you enjoy them when they were happening?"

"I really did," I nodded. "That's something I've always been thankful for. After Greg and your dad were killed I never found myself thinking 'I wish I'd appreciated them more when they were alive...' or anything like that. I really did appreciate everything when it was happening. You need to do the same thing."

"I'll try," she said, but she still didn't look convinced.

That night I told Laci about my conversation with Charlotte...she was *very* interested.

"Wow!" she said. "I can't believe it! That sounds just like what happened to me."

"Not really," I said, shaking my head. "She doesn't like Jordan *at all*."

"Well," she said, "I didn't like you at all either."

"Oh, you did too," I said, waving my hand at her dismissively.

"No, I didn't," she said, laughing. "Where'd you get an idea like that?"

"From you!" I said. "You said you liked me ever since preschool!"

"That's not what I told you," she argued. "God told me you were the one for me when I was in preschool. I never said I was happy about it."

I looked at her with my mouth open.

"You honestly thought I *liked* you...as mean as you were to me all the time?"

I rolled my eyes at her.

"You liked me by the time you were Charlotte's age."

"No, I didn't..." she said.

"Yes, you did...Greg told me you did."

"Well," she said, shaking her head. "If Greg told you that then he lied to you."

I started thinking back.

"Did he ask you to a dance in the seventh grade?"

She nodded at me.

"Okay," I said. "Well, he told me that he asked you and you wouldn't go with him because you liked somebody else. That was me...*right*?"

"Sorry," she said, shaking her head again. "I never told him that."

"Why didn't you go with Greg then?"

"Well," she said, "Greg and I were already pretty good friends by then and I really liked him a lot..."

"You liked him?"

"Of course I did," she said.

"You mean you liked him as a friend, right?"

"Well, no," she said. "I mean I *liked* him, liked him."

"Greg? You liked *Greg*?"

"What was there not to like?" she asked, grinning. "He was funny and he had such a heart for God and he was so *cute*..."

"I never noticed," I said dryly and she laughed.

"And David!" she said, excitement growing in her eyes. "He started growing his hair out just so he could send it to Locks of Love! I mean he was like a man after my own heart! How could I NOT like him?"

"I cannot believe this..." I said, shaking my head.

"You're not *jealous*, are you?" she asked, an impish look on her face.

"I'm not sure," I admitted. "You do like *me* now...right?"

"You're okay..."

"*Anyway*," I said. "So, why didn't you go to the dance with him then?"

"Well," she said, "I had pretty much spent the past eight or nine years pretty unhappy with the idea that I was supposed to be with you and when Greg moved to town I was pretty certain that God had made a mistake and that Greg was really the one for me...I mean, he was so *perfect*..."

"Yeah," I said, rolling my eyes again. "I got that part. Keep going..."

She smiled and I decided she was enjoying this *way* too much.

"So, when he asked me to the dance I said yes and-"

"You said *YES?*"

"Uh-huh," she nodded and smiled again.

"Go on..." I sighed.

"Well," she said. "One day I made some remark about how I wished he wasn't friends with you and he asked me why I let you bother me so much and...I don't know. It just kind of came out. I basically wound up telling him what God had told me...just like Charlotte did with you this morning."

"Then what?"

"Then Greg said we shouldn't go to the dance together...he just totally backed off. I said I thought we should still go, but he didn't think it was a good idea. He said that if God had spoken to me that I had to be obedient to that – no matter what I thought or felt and no matter what you did. He said you were God's problem – not mine – and that God would see to it that you'd come around...*eventually*."

We were both quiet for a moment.

"Greg was a really good friend to me for all those years," Laci said. "He was just very encouraging and helped me have faith...especially after I *did* start to have feelings for you."

"When was that?" I asked.

"It was gradual," she said, smiling. "When we came down here on our mission trip I decided that maybe you weren't so bad after all. And then you started helping me in math and you finally apologized to me for being so mean when we were little...that's when I really started to fall for you."

She kissed me and sat back, still smiling.

"When did you start having feelings for me?" she wanted to know.

"I'm still waiting for them."

"Oh, come on!" she said, swatting at me. "Tell me."

"Well," I said, winding a strand of her hair around my finger. "It was really gradual for me too. I guess after our mission trip is when I decided to stop being mean to you because I really began to appreciate your heart and then over then next couple of years we started becoming really close friends and I cared about you a lot..."

"But just as a friend, right?" she asked.

"Well, yeah," I admitted. "But a really, really good friend...one of my *best* friends..."

"So," she said. "When did you start feeling something more?"

"I guess prom night..."

"Seeing me with Tanner?" she grinned.

"Well, sort of," I said.

She nodded.

"Yet another good-looking guy who stepped out of the way to make room for you."

"What are you talking about?"

"Yeah," she said. "He asked me to the prom and I told him it would have to be just as friends because I liked somebody else and he rolled his eyes at me and said: 'Let me guess...*David*?' and I nodded. He said we should go anyway...that maybe it would shake some sense into you if you saw what you were missing. I guess he was right, huh?"

"Well, sort of," I said again. "But really, it started earlier that night."

"I didn't even see you earlier..."

"When I was out to dinner with Samantha," I said.

"Oh?" Her face clouded slightly and I sensed an opportunity for payback.

"Well," I continued. "Talk about your good-looking prom dates. You remember what *Samantha* looked like, right?"

"Uh-huh," Laci said without much enthusiasm.

"Do you remember her *hair*? She had *great* hair! Remember?"

"You're obsessed with hair, aren't you?" Laci asked, not smiling.

"Possibly," I grinned, tugging at the strand I'd been twirling around my finger. She swatted my hand away.

"Oh!" I said. "I get it! It's fine for you to tell me how cute Greg was and how nice-looking Tanner is, but if I start talking about how pretty Sam is then suddenly you don't want to have this conversation anymore – is that right?"

"Do you think she's prettier than me?" Laci asked in a quiet voice.

Not by a long shot...not even close. That was the truth and that's what I *should* have said, but instead, I teased her.

"Well, she probably doesn't have a big ol' belly like you do..."

Laci burst into tears.

Hormones...

"Oh, stop it Laci. I'm just kidding. Stop!" I put my arms around her. "No one is prettier than you...*no one.* You're the most beautiful woman in the world and you know that. You know what the most beautiful part of you is?"

"What?" she managed to sniff.

"Your big ol' belly," I said, patting it with one hand. "I wouldn't change anything about you at all, but especially not that."

I might as well have been saying *blah, blah, blah* because she kept on crying.

Two and a half more months...

"Laci...listen," I said, shaking her shoulder. "You wanna know how pretty I thought you were back then?"

"How?" she sniffed.

"Remember when we danced together at the Valentine's dance when we were freshmen?"

She nodded.

"Do you know why I danced with you?"

"Because you promised Greg that you'd dance with the next girl who asked you and you were trying to make Sam jealous."

She was making this impossible.

"Okay," I admitted, "but I was really glad that *you're* the one who asked me. Do you know why?"

"Why?"

"Because," I said, tipping her chin up and turning her face toward me. "You were the prettiest girl there...you were beautiful. You still are."

She managed a smile and wiped a tear away.

"Now," I said, "do you want to hear the rest of the story? Do you want to know why I fell in love with *you*?"

She nodded.

"You have to stop crying," I said.

"I have stopped," she sniffled again.

"I took her out to eat..."

"Where'd you take her?"

"McDonald's..."

Laci smiled again.

"We went to *Chez Condrez*," I said. "We were eating escargot and she pulled up all of her hair onto one side of her head into a ponytail...you know – like to keep it out of the way?"

Laci nodded.

"And I just looked at her hair and all of a sudden I wondered how many inches long it was and how some little kid would look wearing a wig made out of her hair..."

"That made you start having feelings for me?" she asked skeptically. She didn't look too impressed.

"Don't you see, Laci? No one will ever know how Sam's hair would look on a wig because Sam would never do that! I mean...I don't know, she might, but I doubt it. That's something *you* would do!"

"Sooo," she said, slowly, "you like me because I send my hair to Locks of Love all the time?"

"No," I said, shaking my head. "It's because you're the type of person who would do that and she wasn't. It's like Greg told me one time...Sam didn't have the same heart as me. That's when I started to realize that he was right, and once I realized that, I knew who *did* have the same heart as me."

"You knew it was me?" she asked, finally smiling.

"Well, that's when I started realizing that Greg had been right...that you were the one for me."

The smile dropped off her face again.

"Greg told you that?"

I nodded.

"What else did he tell you?"

"Well, that Sam wasn't the one for me and that you liked me and–"

"He TOLD you that I liked you?!"

I had a feeling those hormones were about to kick in again.

I nodded, very slightly.

"He promised me he would *never* tell you that," Laci said almost in a whisper.

"Well," I said. "Then it looks like he lied to both of us."

We sat quietly for a moment and then she looked at me.

"When did he tell you that I liked you?" she asked.

"Christmas..."

"You knew at *CHRISTMAS*?" she yelled. "You still kept chasing after Sam and you took her to the prom and everything and you *knew* that I liked you the *WHOLE TIME*?!"

"I was an idiot," I said. "I think that's why Greg finally told me – I was being such an idiot and he probably couldn't stand it anymore. It just took me awhile to realize that he was right."

She looked a little happier and I made a mental note to call myself an idiot more often.

"I'm sorry you had to wait for me for so long," I said, not just talking about high school.

"Whatever it took for us to get to where we are..." she said after a moment, "I'm really glad for it."

"And I'm really glad that you listened to God."

"It was worth every minute that I waited."

"You and this baby are everything to me..." I told her quietly. "*Everything*."

"I love you," she said.

"I love you, too."

We went to the airport when it was time for the Cavendish mission group to go home. I gave Charlotte a big hug before she went through security.

"I want to talk to you for a second about Jordan," I said. I saw anger flash in her eyes just at the sound of his name.

"Charlotte...do you know what Greg would say to you if he were here right now?"

She shook her head.

"He'd tell you that you have to be obedient to God. If God told you that Jordan's the one for you, then he is. God will make that happen."

"But I don't even like him..." she said, shaking her head.

"You will," I said. "One day you will."

"Even if I do, he won't ever like me. He hates me!"

"Jordan is God's problem, not your's. You need to have faith and trust God. Jordan will come around one day. Just be patient."

She looked at me doubtfully.

"Trust me, Charlotte," I said. "One day Jordan will thank God for you every day and he'll be so glad that you obeyed what God told you to do."

"Thanks, Davey," she said, hugging me again. "I love you."

"I love you too," I said. "I wish I was there to remind you every day...don't forget what I said, okay? He'll come around."

"I won't forget," she said.

"Promise?"

"I promise."

"I'll see you in six weeks," I said.

"I can't wait!" she answered. And then she was gone.

When Charlotte left to return to Cavendish, Laci was 32 weeks pregnant. I knew that the doctor didn't want Gabby born this early, but I also knew that if a pregnancy could make it to 32 or 33 weeks, the baby had an excellent chance of surviving even if it was born prematurely. That was very comforting to know. There was a whole little person in there...sucking her thumb, opening and closing her eyes, and listening to the world around her.

Every morning and every evening I talked to her and was often rewarded with a strong kick or a punch. If I gently pushed Laci's belly, Gabby would usually push right back, trying to resettle into whatever position she'd been in before I bothered her.

We decided that she was going to be brilliant and would make straight A's in school. Even if she struggled in something, her mom and dad would be able to help her – Laci in anything related to social studies or language and me in math or science.

We both read out loud to her from the Bible and Laci sang to her every day. She tried to get me to sing too.

"I can't sing," I said.

"Oh, you can too," she argued. "You sing to Dorito all the time."

"*What* did you just call him?"

"Doroteo..."

"No you didn't. You just called him Dorito."

"I don't think so," she said.

"Yes, you did," I said, smiling. I was going to be able to rub that in her face for a long time.

We were going to be home for ten weeks.

Ten whole weeks!

Laci's parents picked us up at the airport and I rode up front with Laci's dad while Laci and her mom sat in the back and discussed every detail of the pregnancy. They'd already covered every bit of it over the past few months on the phone, but I guess it was different in person. I looked out the window as we drove along.

"You know what I want to do while we're home this spring?" I asked when there was a lull in the conversation.

"What?"

"Mow grass."

"I can arrange that for you," Laci's dad said and I smiled.

We pulled up at my sister Jessica's house. Jessica lived just a few miles from our old neighborhood. We didn't even get to the porch before the front door swung open.

"Uncle Dave!" my niece, Cassidy, cried as she ran to me. I was glad she hadn't forgotten me.

"Hey there, big girl!" I said, grabbing her and holding her up. "Man! What are they feeding you? You must've grown five inches! What've you been eating?"

"Fish sticks!" she said, smiling.

"Fish sticks?"

She nodded.

"She loves 'em," Jessica said. She was waiting in the doorway and gave me a big hug when I got to her. She had my nephew CJ in her arms. I put Cassidy down and she ran to Laci.

Laci didn't try to pick Cassidy up, but she leaned over and hugged her.

"My cousin's in there," Cassidy said, patting Laci's belly gently. Jessica had prepared her well.

I took CJ from Jessica.

"Hey, little guy," I said, walking into the living room with him. He didn't seem as sure about me as Cassidy had (I hadn't seen him since he was about six months old) and he kept a good eye on his mom.

He was a lot smaller than Dorito.

"Are you walking yet?" I asked him.

"He sure is," Jessica said, taking him from me. She set him down on the carpet and he toddled over to the couch. He turned around and held onto it, observing us.

"Can you stay for a little while?" Jessica was asking Laci's mom and dad.

"We'll at least stay until they get all their luggage downstairs," Laci's dad said. Jessica and her husband, Chris, had their basement already fixed up for company because his parents came to visit from St. Louis from time to time. There was a furnished bedroom and a living room with a couch and a television. It beat staying in my old bedroom or in Laci's.

"What is he?" I asked Jessica, pointing at CJ as he pulled himself up onto the couch. "Thirteen months?"

"Yep."

"Oh," I said. "He walks good."

After Mike had graduated from high school his mom had moved to Minnesota because that's where Mike was going to be going to college and she wanted to be closer to him. As a result Mike didn't make it back to Cavendish too often, but a few days after we'd gotten home he called me and said he'd be in town for the weekend and that he wanted us to get together. He was going to stay with Tanner, so by the time he showed up at Jessica's house to pick up me and Laci, he already had Tanner with him. After many hugs and a lot of pats on Laci's belly, we piled into Mike's car.

"Where are we going?" Mike asked.

"Do you really have to ask?" Tanner wanted to know, glancing back at me.

"No," I said. "It's up to Laci. I've learned to never get between a pregnant woman and her food."

Tanner craned around to look at Laci who was sitting behind him.

"*Hunter's* is fine," she sighed and I smiled at her.

It felt so good to be with old friends in a familiar place, listening to nothing but English.

"When's your baby shower?" Tanner asked Laci.

"Next Saturday afternoon at Ashlyn and Brent's house," she answered. "Natalie's coming in from Colorado for it."

"Tell her I said hi," Mike said.

"Me too," Tanner added.

"Why don't you come tell her yourself?" I asked them.

"To a *baby* shower?" Tanner asked, raising his eyebrow. "I don't think so."

"*I* have to be there," I mumbled. "Come on. It'll be fun. *Really*."

"Gee whiz," Tanner said, "that *does* sound like a blast, but the baseball team has their first away game that day."

"Can I come help?" I begged. Laci swatted me. I looked pleadingly at Mike next.

"Wanna come?"

"Sorry," he said. "I'm on a tight schedule...I'm lucky to be here now."

"I heard you got into med school," Laci told him. "Congratulations!"

"Thanks," he smiled.

"Speaking of med school," I said, "I've been meaning to ask you something. What do you know about rickets?"

"Rickets?" He looked puzzled. "I don't think you see a lot of that anymore...it's mostly due to poor nutrition...lack of vitamin D I think."

"What about the long term prognosis though...if someone gets rickets?"

"I'm not sure," Mike answered. "I'm not *in* med school yet and I really don't know much about rickets."

"I know about rickets," Tanner said and we all stared at him.

"What? How come everybody always acts like I'm a big, dumb jock?"

"Hmmm, I wonder..." Mike said, rubbing his chin thoughtfully.

"Very funny," Tanner replied. "A major in athletic sciences is a lot more demanding than most people realize..."

"I'm sure it is," I nodded dramatically.

"I'm serious. I bet if you had a cardiac arrest right now I could resuscitate you a lot faster than *doctor* Mike here could."

"Oh, *please*," Mike said. "I'm an EMT..."

"Forget it," I said. "Just let me die. I don't want either one of you giving me mouth-to-mouth."

They all laughed.

"So, anyway," I said to Tanner, "what do you know about rickets?"

"O.J. Simpson had rickets when he was a little kid and he had to wear leg braces."

"O.J. Simpson?"

Tanner nodded.

"Fantastic," I said. "That'll be a great role model for Dorito."

"Dorito?" Mike asked.

"Yeah," I said. "He's this kid at the orphanage where Laci works. He had rickets and his legs are bowed out now because of it."

"His name's *Dorito*?" Tanner asked, incredulous.

"Yeah–"

"*NO!*" Laci interrupted. "His name is *NOT* Dorito! His name is Doroteo. David's just too stubborn to call him by his right name."

"It's his nickname," I said. "He loves it."

"It's a *stupid* nickname," Laci murmured.

"It's a great nickname!" I argued.

"It's not even a nickname...it's a *snack food*."

"Remember that guy in the band who was a few grades ahead of us?" Tanner asked. "His name was Chip..."

"That's *exactly* what I told Laci!" I said, beaming at him.

"There was this guy in my freshman dorm named Oreo," Mike chimed in.

"Please don't encourage him," Laci said, looking dismayed.

"Dorito's a great nickname," I said again. "Admit it."

She shook her head in disgust.

"Whatchya gonna call the baby?" Mike wanted to know. "Cheeto?"

"How about Frito?" Tanner suggested.

“Don’t give him any ideas,” Laci begged.

“So, anyway,” I said. “Are you serious? OJ had rickets?”

“Yup,” Tanner said. “And then he went on to become one of the greatest running backs of all time...”

“Among other things...” Mike muttered under his breath.

“What about Forrest Gump?” Laci asked, looking at Mike. “Is that why he wore leg braces?”

“I don’t have any idea,” Mike said.

“Forrest wasn’t a real person, dear,” I reminded her, patting her hand.

“Actually they called Venus Lacey the Forrest Gump of our 1996 women’s Olympic basketball team,” Tanner said. “She had to wear leg braces when she was little because her legs were so twisted when she was born that her feet were practically pointing backwards. There’ve been a lot of real people who’ve had serious problems with their legs when they were little and they’ve gone on to be great athletes...”

“I want to know some more of them,” I told Tanner.

“Umm...besides OJ?”

“Yes, please.” I raised an eyebrow at him.

“Okay, let me think...” he said. “Well, Tom Dempsy was born missing part of his foot and he went on to become a kicker in the NFL...”

“Really?”

“Uh-huh...and Wilma Rudolph had polio when she was little – she had to wear leg braces too. She was on our Olympic track team in...1960 I think, and she won three gold medals.”

“That makes me feel better...maybe Dorito’ll be okay.” I turned to Mike. “Remember Miguel?”

Mike nodded.

“Who’s Miguel?” Laci asked, looking perplexed.

“He was this guy we met at the landfill when we were on our mission trip,” Mike told her.

“I don’t remember him,” Laci said.

“You didn’t meet him,” I said. “He didn’t come up to the bus...”

“How come I’ve never heard about him?”

“It’s not a lot of fun to talk about,” Mike explained.

"Oh..."

"Something was wrong with one of his legs and his foot," I said. "It was all..."

"Withered," Mike finished for me and I nodded.

Laci looked at Tanner.

"The culture down there is..." she hesitated, "different. It's easy for someone with a handicap like that to wind up..."

"Living in a *landfill*," I said as our waitress set two large pizzas down at our table.

"I'm going to have such bad heartburn," Laci complained, reaching for a slice of pizza.

"Have you been having a lot of heartburn since you've been pregnant?" Mike asked her.

"Uh-huh," she nodded. "I have to buy the economy-sized jars of Rolaids."

"You know what that means, don't ya?" Mike asked.

"What?" We both looked at him, expecting to hear some great medical wisdom come from his mouth.

"The baby's going to have a lot of hair."

"Oh, brother," Laci said.

We said grace and began eating. The pizza tasted exactly the same way it had in high school. It was great.

"So why'd you bring up Miguel?" Mike asked. "Did you see him again or something?"

"No," I said, shaking my head, "but when I found out about Dorito's legs it made me think of him and I just got worried that Dorito might wind up the same way..."

"So David got him orthotics and takes him to physical therapy," Laci said.

"How's that going?" Mike asked.

"Good," I said. "I just hope they keep up with his exercises while I'm gone."

"Do you go to the landfill very much?" Mike asked me.

"No," I said, "but Laci goes all the time."

"Charlotte told me it was pretty bad," Tanner commented.

"It is," I agreed. "Speaking of Charlotte...how is she?"

"Good," he said. "It's kind of weird teaching her and Jordan every day..."

"How's Jordan doing?" Laci asked.

"Okay, I guess," he shrugged, not acting as if Jordan was doing okay at all.

"What's wrong?"

"I had to kick him off the baseball team."

"Why?"

"He's flunking math..."

"I can relate," Laci said.

"I wish I lived here," I told Tanner. "I'd help him."

"Those were the days," Laci smiled.

"Yeah," Tanner said, reaching for another piece of pizza. "You two always pretending like you were studying math..."

"We *were* studying math!" I said.

"Uh-huh."

"We *were*, weren't we, Laci?"

"I was trying..." she smiled again.

"No, you weren't," Tanner scoffed. "The only thing you were trying to do was get David's attention."

Laci just smiled some more.

"What a dope you were," Tanner said to me. "The prettiest girl in school and you were just so...so *oblivious*!"

"Easy there with the vocabulary, big guy," I said. "I wouldn't want you to strain something."

"It does seem awfully unfair," Mike added. "How did someone like *you* wind up with someone like *her*?"

"I've always had a thing for pathetic guys," Laci offered.

"That's all it would have taken?" Tanner asked, his mouth dropping open. "I just needed to act pathetic?"

"Mental note," Mike said quietly. "Act pathetic."

"You want her?" I asked them. "You can have her! Go ahead...one of you take her now...*quick!* Before she goes into labor!"

"If I take her now do I have to go to the baby shower on Saturday?" Tanner asked.

"It's a package deal," I nodded. "The baby shower, the hormones, the smart-mouth..."

They all laughed and Laci squeezed my knee under the table.

After the pizza was gone we ordered strawberry cheesecake. While we were waiting for it to arrive I looked at Tanner.

"Hey, Tanner," I said. "I've been wondering about something..."

"What?" He was swirling his straw around in his drink.

"Remember this?" I asked, holding up my hand for him to see. I pinched my thumb and forefinger together, as if I were holding something tiny, like a grain of salt. Greg had always done that to Tanner, but he'd never tell me why. Tanner looked up at me and suppressed a laugh.

"Yeah," he said. "I remember it..."

"What's it mean?"

"Nothing," Tanner said, concentrating on his straw again. He put his finger over the end of it, lifted it over his glass, and then removed his finger, watching the liquid dribble back into his glass. We all stared at him until he looked back up.

"Come on, Tanner," Mike finally said. "You might as well tell us."

Tanner sighed.

"He was just pretending that he was holding up a spider," Tanner said, shrugging. "That's all."

"There's gotta be more to it than that," I said.

"This oughta be good," Mike said.

Tanner kept playing with his straw.

"Let's hear it," Laci pressed.

"Fine," he said, shaking his head. "One day Greg found this spider in the gym and I guess he thought it was *cool* or something so he picked it up by one leg and showed it to me."

"*And?*" I asked.

"And I don't like spiders..."

"*And?*"

"And that's it," Tanner said.

"Did you scream like a girl?" Mike teased.

"*He shoved it in my face!*"

"You did, didn't you?" I laughed. "You screamed like a girl!"

"I was in the *seventh* grade!" Tanner protested.

“Were you scared of the whittle spider?” Mike asked in a high-pitched voice, tickling the back of Tanner’s neck with his fingers.

“Stop it!” he said, slapping Mike’s hand away. Then he shuddered. “Ughhhh! Spiders!”

Mike and I were laughing. Laci was too, but not quite as hard.

“Don’t feel bad, Tanner,” she said. “Everybody’s afraid of something. I’m scared to death of rats.”

This was actually pretty significant since she went to the landfill twice a week.

“I’m not scared of anything,” Mike said.

“Yeah, *right!*” Tanner and I both said at the same time.

“What?” he asked defensively just before a knowing look came over his face. “Oh...yeah.”

“What?” Laci asked.

“Snakes,” I whispered.

“It was *in* my sleeping bag,” Mike complained and we all laughed.

“What about you?” Tanner asked me. “What are *you* afraid of?”

“Pregnant women who don’t get their dessert,” I said, looking around for our waitress. “Where’s our cheesecake?”

After dessert we lingered at our table until the cashier politely told us that they *really* wanted to close. Mike and Tanner insisted on splitting the bill and Laci went into the restroom while they headed to the cash register by the front door.

On the wall, not far from our table, was a plaque that the owner had hung shortly after Greg had died. It had his senior picture on it (the same one that was hanging in my office in Mexico), and mentioned the dates that he had worked at *Hunter’s*. I was standing there, looking at it, when Laci came out of the bathroom.

“You ready to go?” I asked, turning toward her.

She nodded and reached for my hand.

“I had a great time tonight,” she said. “Did you?”

I nodded, smiled at her, and glanced at Greg’s picture one last time.

“It was almost perfect.”

She squeezed my hand and smiled back and then we turned to head for the door.

Laci was usually asleep when I woke up, so I was surprised the next morning when I opened my eyes to find her lying next to me, wide awake.

Her hands were on her belly.

"Good morning," I said.

"Something's wrong," she said, casting an anxious glance my way.

"What do you mean?"

"She's not moving," Laci said, panic creeping into her voice. "I can't feel her moving."

"She's running out of room," I said. "You know they say the baby doesn't move as much right before it's born."

"She's not moving *at all*," Laci's eyes filled with tears. "Something's wrong."

I propped myself up on one elbow and put my hand on Laci's belly. I pushed gently, moved my hand back and forth and put my mouth near my hand.

"Hey, baby," I said. "Wake up, Gabby. Your momma's gettin' all worried."

I laid my head on Laci's belly, waiting to feel Gabby kick at me or poke me with her fist, but I felt nothing.

"Do you feel anything?" Laci asked in a strangled voice.

"No," I admitted, "but they quit moving around so much toward the end. Don't let yourself get so upset."

But Laci was already upset.

"Do you want me to call Dr. Sedevick and make sure this is normal?" I asked. Laci nodded and I reached for my phone.

Dr. Sedevick actually answered her office line. I told her who I was and what was going on.

"When's the last time she felt the baby move?" Dr. Sedevick asked.

"Laci?" I asked. "When's the last time you felt her move?"

"Last night..."

"Last night," I told Dr. Sedevick.

"Well," Dr. Sedevick answered, "the baby's getting very crowded in there...they tend to slow down their movements a lot right before birth, so it's probably nothing to be worried about..."

"That's what I told her," I said, smiling at Laci.

"Can you bring her by this morning? We'll just take a listen and make sure everything's okay...put Laci's mind at ease."

"Sure," I said. "When?"

"I'm scheduled to be at the hospital at noon," she said. "Anytime between now and then will be fine. It won't take but a few seconds."

"Thanks," I said and I closed my phone.

"She said to get you on in there so she can convince you everything's okay," I said. "It's not good for you to be getting all worked up."

"Now?" Laci asked.

"Any time between now and lunchtime."

"I want to go now," Laci replied.

"Okay."

Tears were running down her face the entire way to the doctor's office. I kept trying to convince her that everything was going to be fine and she kept on nodding, but the tears didn't stop.

We didn't have to sit very long in the waiting area before we were called back into an examination room. I helped Laci get onto the examination table and then I took a chair near her head. I was holding her hand when Dr. Sedevick came in.

"Good morning, Laci," Dr. Sedevick said, smiling at her and nodding at me. I nodded back to her and Laci said good morning in a quiet voice.

"Still haven't felt her move?"

Laci shook her head.

"Happens all the time," Dr. Sedevick said, patting Laci's other hand before she put her stethoscope in her ears. "Let's see if we can put your mind at ease. Okay?"

Laci nodded.

The doctor lifted Laci's maternity shirt and put the stethoscope to her belly. Laci closed her eyes.

The doctor moved the stethoscope from one spot to another, listening intently. She looked at Laci, saw that her eyes were closed, and then she looked at me. There was no comfort in her face.

"Margaret," she said to the nurse who was hanging by the door. "Why don't you bring the cart in here?"

The cart was the portable sonogram machine. Dr. Sedevick squirted a blob of jelly on Laci's belly and began pressing the little wand onto her skin.

"Have you been having any pain, Laci?"

"No." Almost a whisper. Eyes still closed.

"Any bleeding or unusual discharge?"

Laci didn't open her eyes, but she shook her head.

The monitor was turned so that Laci couldn't see it, but I moved myself around so that I could. I'd watched our home footage enough to recognize Gabby's spine. I kept watching for the beating of her little heart, but I couldn't find it. Dr. Sedevick looked at me, bit her lip, and shook her head. She put the wand back on the cart, pushed it toward Margaret and wiped the clear jelly off of Laci's skin. She pulled Laci's shirt down and took Laci's other hand.

"Laci?" she said. "Laci?"

Tears began *pouring* down Laci's cheeks.

"I'm very sorry," Dr. Sedevick began, and then Laci *really* started crying. "There's nothing that could have been done to prevent this...sometimes it just happens. I'm so very sorry."

Margaret opened the door and wheeled the sonogram cart into the hall. I panicked for a moment watching it go, feeling as if she was somehow taking Gabby away. But then I remembered that Gabby was still here...with Laci.

Dr. Sedevick continued talking.

"We're going to need to admit you into the hospital, Laci. It can be anytime today or tomorrow, but I wouldn't feel comfortable waiting any longer than that."

Laci did nothing but cry, so Dr. Sedevick turned to me.

"Today," I said quietly. Dr. Sedevick nodded.

"I'll give you a few minutes and I'll be back," she said. She patted Laci's hand one more time.

"I'm very sorry," Dr. Sedevick said one more time. Then she left and closed the door.

Margaret came back in.

"Would you like to come into the office?" she asked. "You'll be more comfortable..."

We both helped Laci off of the examination table and into Dr. Sedevick's office. There was a couch and we helped her sit down on it. I sat next to her and Margaret left us alone.

"I'm sorry, Laci," I said, holding her against me while she sobbed. "I'm so, so sorry."

We sat there and cried for a while, and then I realized we had to let our parents know. I called my mom first.

"Hi, honey," she answered the phone.

"Mom..." I said. My voice broke and I think she probably heard Laci crying in the background too.

"David," she said. "Is the baby all right?"

"No..."

"Oh, David," she said, her voice catching. "What's wrong?"

I couldn't answer her.

"Is she...is she not *going* to be all right?"

"No," I said.

"Oh, honey," she said. "I'm so sorry. What can I do?"

"We have to go to the hospital," I began.

"You want me to bring Laci's bag?" she asked. "Have you called Laci's parents?"

"No..."

"Do you want me to go over there and tell them?"

"Yes," I said, grateful that someone could pull it together enough to be in control. "Thank you."

"I'm sorry, David," she said again. "I'm so, so sorry."

Everybody was sorry.

Everybody was so very, very sorry.

Sitting on the couch, holding Laci as she sobbed, I started to get really concerned about her – she was pretty much hysterical. My first thought was that it couldn't be good for the baby for her to get so upset, but then I caught myself and just worried about Laci. Dr. Sedevick finally came into the office and asked if we were ready to head over to the hospital.

"Can you...can you give her something?" I asked. "Something to calm her down?"

Dr. Sedevick shook her head.

"I'm hesitant to give her anything that might compromise her ability to assist with labor..."

Assist with labor?

I don't know what I'd thought was going to happen when we got to that hospital, but not until right then did I realized that Laci was still going to have to go through the entire birthing process, just as if Gabby were still alive.

How?

How was she ever going to do that?

How she was able to do that (it turns out) is that they broke her water and pumped Pitocin into her veins until her body was wracked with such painful contractions that she couldn't *not* push and she screamed and cried with pain and grief.

Of course, when Gabby was finally born I was hoping that the doctor's instruments had been wrong and that it had all been a big mistake, and that Gabby would let out a lusty cry and prove to everybody what a strong and healthy little girl she really was and how everybody had been wrong about her.

But it was silent in the room when she was born.

Absolutely silent.

The only sound was a nurse announcing the time of her birth: 7:34 p.m. It was just after that that Laci, mercifully, finally fell asleep.

They wheeled Laci into a regular room – away from the maternity ward where all the other mommies were with their babies and their flowers and their balloons. Laci woke up in the middle of the night when a nurse came in to check on her. I had fallen asleep too, seated in a chair with my head on Laci's hospital bed, near her shoulder. I woke up when she did.

"Please tell me this is all a bad dream," she whispered to me and I pressed my face into her hair, against her neck and pillow.

The nurse looked at us both.

"When you lose a baby," she said, "you need a chance to say goodbye. We have her all ready for you to see...I can bring her in whenever you'd like."

I was very surprised. I'd caught a glimpse of Gabby after she'd been born and I didn't know I'd get to see her again. Laci, however, didn't seem surprised at all.

"Now," Laci said. "I want to see her right now please."

The nurse nodded and left the room.

"I just want to see her," Laci sobbed. "I just want to see her."

I stroked her hair and she kept crying until the nurse came back into the room.

Gabby was wrapped up in a soft, white blanket with only her face showing. Laci reached up and took her from the nurse and the nurse left us alone with our baby. Laci stroked Gabby's face with her fingertip and kissed her nose and forehead. She talked to Gabby and lifted the blanket from the top of her head.

"Look at her hair, David," Laci said to me. "*Look* at her hair..."

I looked. It seemed freshly washed and was the same color as Laci's.

"Look how much hair she has," Laci said, almost in awe. "I can't believe how much hair she has."

I leaned over and kissed Gabby's hair. It smelled clean too. I wondered whose job it was to make sure that little babies who had died looked and smelled nice for their parents who had to say goodbye before they'd even said hello.

"Do you want to hold her?"

I took Gabby from Laci and sat on the edge of the bed with her. It was too much for me to stand.

I looked at her little face and was mesmerized by her lips. I couldn't believe how perfectly shaped they were. There was a tiny little mark on her upper lip and I knew it was a blister from sucking her thumb. I couldn't get over how perfect her lips were. I traced them with my fingertip.

I pulled the blanket back and took one of her hands between my fingers. I laid my index finger under her hand – against her palm – and used my thumb to wrap her fingers around mine. Her fingers were perfect too.

After a while I kissed her perfect little lips and gave her back to her mother. I'm not sure how long we had her before the nurse came in and took her away from us, but the moment that she left with Gabby was the worst moment of all.

Before Laci was discharged from the hospital, I talked with the pediatrician who had examined Gabby after she was born. I wanted to know – medically – why she had died.

"She had an umbilical cord anomaly," he told me. "She basically wasn't getting the nutrients that she needed."

Laci had spent almost a year traipsing to the landfill to feed hungry kids. The irony of this was not lost on me.

"There's nothing that could have been done to prevent it," he added.

I nodded, wondering why everybody always thought the fact that nothing could have been done to prevent it was somehow supposed to make it better.

Laci was a mess before the funeral and her parents took care of her while my parents and I made the funeral arrangements. I was looking at the different coffins and trying to make decisions when my dad told me that he was going to be paying all the expenses. I started to protest, but he stopped me, and in an instant I knew to let him do what he could to help. I concentrated instead on picking out what we would want for Gabby.

Ashlyn was supposed to be in charge of the baby shower, but instead she helped with the funeral arrangements. She talked to me, tried talking to Laci, and relayed things to the minister for us. It was Ashlyn's idea to play a song by Watermark at Gabby's funeral. I had been listening to Christian music for over ten years and I'd heard songs by Watermark before, but I'd never heard this one. It was the perfect song to play and I was really glad that Ashlyn had thought of it.

It was called *Glory Baby* and it was sung to a little baby who had died. It told her to let Jesus hold her until Mom and Dad would be able to. It made me feel better to think of Jesus holding Gabby until Laci and I were there, but another image came to my mind too. I thought for just a moment about Greg and I pictured him holding my daughter and running his finger over her perfect little lips. When he smiled at her, I saw her smile back.

That made me feel better too.

Physically Laci still had to go through the same healing process that any woman goes through after giving birth, but usually they have a wonderful, healthy little baby to take their mind off of all the pain and discomfort that their body goes through. All Laci had to take her mind off of the *physical* pain was additional emotional and mental pain – the same pain that I was going through. It took all the prayers of our friends and family to get us through.

As the days wore on and slowly turned into weeks, we cried a little less and began trying to focus our minds on returning to Mexico. One week before we were set to leave, however, I suddenly remembered that we had reserved a third seat for Gabby.

A third seat.

An empty seat beside us on the entire flight back.

I went into the backyard so that Laci couldn't hear me call the airline.

"I need to relinquish a ticket, please," I told the lady who answered my call. She asked me for the reservation number and pulled our information onto her computer.

"Sir," she said. "These tickets are non-refundable."

"I know," I said. "I don't care about getting my money back, we just don't need the seat and I was hoping you could fill it."

"I'm sorry, sir," she said. "If you'd purchased the insurance with them we'd be able to reassign your seat, but since you didn't, there's nothing I can do."

"I don't want my money back," I explained again. "I just don't need the seat and I want you to fill it...I want to relinquish the extra seat."

"I'm sorry sir," she said. "There's nothing I can do."

I closed my phone. I usually tried to avoid asking God for favors, but I asked for one now.

Please, God. Please don't make us sit next to an empty seat for the entire flight back to Mexico. Please don't make us be reminded of what we already aren't going to be able to forget anyway...

I hit redial and a different woman answered my call.

"My wife and I are scheduled to fly out on flight 3847 to Mexico City on Tuesday," I said. "We came home to have our baby, but our baby died and we don't need the extra seat and I was hoping..."

"What is your reservation number, sir?" she asked.

"I don't want my money back..."

"What's your reservation number, sir?" she asked again.

I read off the numbers to her.

I could hear her tapping on her keyboard and then she was silent for a moment as she apparently studied our reservations.

"Sir?"

"I just want to relinquish our seat..."

"I understand that, sir," she said. "The coach section has three seats in each row on the right hand side of the aisle and two on the left. I'm trying to see if there's a pair of seats on the left..."

"If you could just fill the third seat..."

"First class only has two seats on either side of the aisle," she went on, ignoring me. "Here's a pair of seats...give me a minute."

I could hear her tapping away some more.

"Sir?"

"Yes?"

"I have you and your wife seated side by side in the first class section. There will be no seat next to either one of you...empty or otherwise."

I wanted to say thank you, but the words stuck in my throat.

"I'm very sorry for your loss, sir," she said. And then, in a whisper, she said, "I'll be praying for you."

I hoped our call wasn't being recorded for "quality assurance purposes" because I was fairly certain that she'd get fired if anyone heard her saying that to me.

"Thank you so much," I whispered back and I was glad that the words didn't get stuck in my throat that time.

Sunday, two days before we were to fly out, Mike came to say goodbye – it was the only chance he was going to have before we left.

After he'd talked with us for a while and hugged Laci, he nodded his head toward the door so I walked him out and stood with him in the driveway next to his car.

"I just wanted to talk to you about something," he said. "It's none of my business, but..."

"What?"

"I just...I just want you to keep an extra careful eye on Laci," he began. "I mean, I know you will anyway, but I want to make sure you understand that she's at high risk for developing clinical depression..."

I crossed my arms and leaned back against his car.

"Fantastic," I said, nodding my head. "That sounds *exactly* like what we need to have happen next. That's just great."

He looked at me as if uncertain whether or not to continue.

"Go on," I sighed.

"You've heard of postpartum depression," he said, waiting for me to nod, which I did. "Well, she obviously has some level of risk because of that...but anytime someone loses a child they're at risk for depression. Laci has two strikes against her...I just want you to really watch her."

"What do I watch for?"

"It's hard to say," he said. "Both of you are going to be grieving and it might be hard for you to tell what's normal and what's not. I'm talking about a biochemical imbalance...something she won't have any control over. You're going to have to really pay attention to her and you're going to have to listen to your gut if you think she's not doing all right."

"Okay."

"Just call me," he said. "You know I'll help you any way I can..."

I nodded and could feel tears spring into my eyes.

He hugged me and patted me on the back.

"I'm really sorry," he said.

I hugged him back and nodded again.

The next night – Monday night – the night before we were to leave, God talked to me for the first time in my life. Maybe He speaks to some people regularly...*but me?* It was something I'd never experienced before.

Like I'd told Charlotte, God had led me before...guided me, spoken to me through Scriptures or songs...stuff like that. But I'd never had anything like this happen to me. It wasn't a voice, but it was more than a feeling. I just somehow *knew* that it was God and that He was telling me something.

It was overwhelming.

Laci was packing in the basement and I was upstairs in the living room, flipping through the newspaper, when it happened. My eyes fell on an ad for an adoption agency.

It was called Adoption Alternatives and it was an agency that specialized (according to their ad) in open adoptions – adoptions where the birth parents and the adoptive parents get to know each other and can stay in touch after the baby is born.

I was looking at it and idly thinking that if I was ever going to adopt I certainly wouldn't want the birth parents sticking around afterward and being a part of our lives. That's when I suddenly felt God telling me something: *You need to call them.*

I looked over at Chris who was reading a magazine. He seemed totally unaware of what had just happened. I looked back at the ad.

I did not *want* to call them. I did not *want* to adopt a baby and have the birth mom (and maybe the dad) visiting on birthdays and at Christmas.

Maybe God was telling me we were supposed to adopt...but through Adoption Alternatives in Cavendish? I didn't think so. I mean Laci *worked* at an orphanage...

Call them.

Okay. Now that was very clear. *Wow...*

The fact that God was clearly telling me something was so powerful that I completely forgot that I didn't want to have a birth mom visiting her biological baby in our home and I forgot that we had non-refundable tickets to fly to Mexico the next day. I jumped out of my chair and bounded down the steps to the basement.

"Laci!" I said, thrusting the newspaper in front of her. "Look!"

She put a shirt in her suitcase and took the paper from me.

I pointed at the ad. She read it and frowned.

"I want to have my own baby," she said, looking at me with dismay.

"We need to call them!"

"No!" she said, almost shouting. "Even if I *was* going to adopt I wouldn't adopt some *white* baby from Cavendish when there are hundreds of kids in Mexico who need us."

She said the word *white* with such venom in her voice that I almost felt ashamed that *I* was white.

"I cannot believe you'd even suggest this," she said, throwing the paper onto the bed and starting to cry.

"No, Laci," I said, wanting to explain. "We just need to call them..."

"NO!" she said. "I told you I don't want to call them! I don't want to adopt a baby! What is *wrong* with you? We just lost Gabby! How can you even *think* about doing this?"

She was crying harder now and the excitement I'd felt from having God tell me something was slipping away fast.

"I just...I just wanted to call them...please don't cry, Laci. Please stop."

She didn't stop.

"I'm sorry," I went on. "We don't have to call them. I made a mistake...I'm sorry. I don't want to call them. Please stop crying."

"I just want to go back to Mexico and try to get on with our lives," she sobbed.

"Me too," I said, wrapping my arms around her. "I'm sorry I said anything."

By the time she stopped crying all the exhilaration I'd felt was gone and I'd convinced myself that God did not really want me to call them after all.

And after that, He didn't talk to me again.

About two months after we returned to Mexico I called Mike.

"Hi, David," he said. "What's up?"

"Am I catching you at a bad time?"

"No," he said. "This is a good time actually...I've got about seven minutes."

Tight schedule.

I got right to it.

"How do I know when Laci's bad enough to make her go to the doctor?"

"Well," he said, "just the fact that you're calling me and asking me that tells me that things have probably already gotten to that point. What's going on?"

"She's not happy. Anything sets her off. She cries all the time. She goes and works with those little kids everyday and it use to make her so happy, but now it just makes her sad. I mean, I'm sad too, but I'm getting better every day...I don't think she is."

"Take her," Mike said. "Make her go. It's treatable...they can do something about it..."

"She's not going to want to take any medicine," I said. "She wants to get pregnant again..."

"There are so many things out there now," he said. "A lot of them she can take when she's pregnant. Plus, sometimes you just need to be on them for a few months to get your serotonin levels back where they need to be and then you can go off of 'em and be fine..."

"Okay," I said.

"And David?"

"What?"

"If the first thing they give her doesn't work don't give up. There're a lot of different options. It may take a while to find the right thing..."

"Are my seven minutes up?" I asked.

"You need anything else?"
"No," I said. "I just wanted to say thanks."
"You're welcome," he said. "Anytime."

I sat her down and told her that I was worried about her and I told her everything Mike had said. She cried some more, but she nodded. I think she knew she needed help.

We went to see Dr. Santos. He prescribed something for her and I called Mike as soon as we picked up the prescription. He didn't answer so I left a voice mail and told him the name of the medicine and asked him to let me know what he thought. I wouldn't let her take the first pill until Mike called me back a few hours later and talked to me in *English.*

"I think it's a good one to start with," he said. "I talked with Dr. Jacobs on staff here and he said it's a common first choice."

I let Laci take her pill.

After about three days her tears dried up, but she complained that her heart was racing at times and she couldn't sleep at night. We gave it two weeks, but decided it wasn't the answer so we went back to Dr. Santos.

The next one he prescribed for her did the trick, and I slowly saw my old Laci coming back to me. She started smiling more often, she got excited about going to work every day, and when we passed a trash can that had a Happy Meal container laying on top she looked at it, but didn't burst into tears.

"Are you sure it's going to be okay for her to be on this if she gets pregnant?" I asked Mike when I called him at the end of the summer.

"I'm positive," he answered. "Are you trying?"
"I guess so."
"Good luck."

In the meantime we got back into what had been our normal routine before we'd gone to Cavendish to have Gabby. While we'd been gone, Aaron had located another church that was willing to take in the youth group kids, so Laci and I got our house back except for the two days a week when the kids from the landfill came.

Dorito was doing great. He'd seemed so happy to see me when I came back from Cavendish...running to me and throwing his arms around my legs. I scooped him up and turned him upside down.

"You haven't forgotten your English, have you?" I'd asked him. He just smiled at me.

"Who am I?" I asked, pointing at myself.

"Day-Day."

"Who are you?" I asked, turning him right side up again and tickling his stomach.

"Dorito," he giggled.

"Good boy," I said.

I kissed him on the top of his head and set him back down.

I started picking him up two or three mornings a week so we could do the exercises that Sonya gave us and then we'd go to McDonald's for lunch afterwards. We were usually able to get there before the lunch crowd and often had the play yard all to ourselves. The ball pit was his favorite part of the entire day.

"Come here!" he called one day, only his head sticking up from the brightly colored balls.

I hated the ball pit.

"What?" I asked, walking over to the black netting that kept him and all the balls inside. He stuck a bare foot into the air.

"Where's your sock?" I asked. He tried to part the balls with his hands, looking for his sock.

"Oh, brother," I said, crawling into the pit.

"Oh, brother," he repeated.

I reached down through the balls, feeling the bottom of the pit. Finally I felt something made of cloth and I pulled up a black sock that almost could have fit me. The next thing I found was a pair of pink underwear with white unicorns printed on it.

"This is disgusting," I said. "Come on, we're getting out."

"Why?" he asked.

"We're going shopping..."

"Why?" he asked again.

"We're going to buy you some new socks."

In early November Laci came into my office and looked over my shoulder. I was checking the weather in Cavendish.

"What's it doing today?" she asked.

"Nothing too much," I said. "They might have a few flurries tomorrow night."

The high in Mexico City that day had been seventy-seven.

"Oh," she said. She sat down on the couch. I twirled in my chair to look at her.

"What's going on?"

"I think maybe I'm pregnant," she said.

"You *think*?" I asked. "*Maybe?*"

She nodded.

"Haven't you taken a test yet?"

She shook her head.

"Why not?"

"I've got one," she said. "I'm going to take it in the morning. You're supposed to take it in the morning..."

"You didn't take it in the morning before..."

"I couldn't wait before," she said. I got out of my chair and sat down next to her, putting my arm around her shoulder.

"I was excited before..."

"You're not excited now?" I asked.

"I'm scared."

"I know," I said. I was probably supposed to tell her to not be scared...that everything was going to be all right. But I was scared too, so I just pulled her closer and kissed the top of her head.

In the morning she crawled back into bed with me and nodded. She put her head on my chest and I wrapped my arms around her, kissing the top of her head again.

"I feel so guilty," she finally said. "No matter what I feel it isn't the right thing. If I'm happy about having another baby then I feel like I'm forgetting about Gabby. If I'm not happy then I feel like I'm cheating this baby."

"I know," I said.

"And I'm so scared," she whispered.

"I know," I said again.

We laid there quietly for a long time and I prayed for God to bring us both comfort and to let us be able to be happy and to enjoy this pregnancy the way we were supposed to. I prayed for Him to take care of this baby and to let it be healthy and for Laci not to have any problems.

But I didn't feel anything or hear a reply back from God...I never did when I prayed anymore.

Ever since I'd disobeyed Him and not called Adoption Alternatives in Cavendish, God had been silent. I *knew* that He was there – I just couldn't feel Him.

I didn't let that stop me from praying to Him though. I just kept reaching out to Him, hoping that one day He'd reach back.

And I wasn't mad at Him – I knew this wasn't His fault.

I was well aware that I was getting exactly what I deserved.

Dr. Santos was able to see us in two days. We figured that Laci was already about eight weeks pregnant so he did an ultrasound and we saw the baby's little heart beating. Laci squeezed my hand and smiled.

No spotting...no bleeding. Laci translated what Dr. Santos told her at the end of our visit.

There's no reason not to expect a completely normal pregnancy and a healthy baby.

Three weeks later though she started bleeding and a rushed trip to see Dr. Santos confirmed what I think we both already knew.

Not this time.

A week after Laci's miscarriage we went on a somber shopping trip together to buy Christmas presents for the orphans. Two weeks after that she told me that she wanted to go off her medication, so I called Mike.

"You really need to talk to her doctor," he said, "but she might do just fine without it now."

"She thinks that's why she lost the baby."

"I don't think so," he said, "but if it's worrying her than it's probably worth trying to get her off of it."

Dr. Santos apparently felt the same way and told her she could stop. After she quit taking it she became weepier than normal, but not as bad as before and I felt that she was handling everything pretty well.

She'd been off of it for four months. The weather website said that Cavendish was experiencing one of the hottest, driest springs on record. You couldn't tell from where we were...it always seemed the same.

In the middle of Cavendish's hot, dry spring, Laci got pregnant again. All of the medicine was completely out of her system, so when she lost that baby in the early summer, I knew it was for some other reason.

By summer, the bowing of Dorito's legs was barely detectable, but he was probably going to need one more set of orthotics before it was all over and I still came and picked him up from the orphanage at least once or twice a week. I brought him to the house to do his exercises and then we'd usually go to McDonald's. I convinced him how much fun it was to go down the tornado slide in the play yard, but the ball pit was still his favorite thing.

We didn't know for sure how old Dorito was, but (based on the other kids I could compare him to) I figured he must be close to three. He could speak to anybody in English or in Spanish now and I was glad. I downloaded educational games off of the Internet for him and ordered a few CDs.

Dorito was smart and I really didn't see any reason why he shouldn't start trying to learn how to read. Sometimes after we finished his exercises we worked on the computer until he got tired of it. Then I'd print off alphabet letters for him so he could lie on the floor of my office and trace them while I corresponded with clients from Argentina to Seattle.

I taped his papers on the wall at eye level for him to look at...underneath all of my snow pictures of Cavendish.

One August morning, Sonya told me that Dorito really didn't need to come see her anymore.

"Keep him active, get him involved in sports...you can keep doing the exercises at home if you'd like, but he really shows no signs of deformity at all. I think once he's through with his last set of braces he's really going to take off."

We went to celebrate at McDonalds.

After we'd eaten our lunch Dorito tore into the ball pit. What his fascination was with that place I'd never know.

“Hey, Dorito,” I said after a few minutes, ignoring the glare from the only other adult who was in the play yard. Apparently Laci had been right...not everyone appreciated a good nickname.

He popped up and looked at me.

“I’m going to the bathroom,” I said. “You stay right here in the ball pit. Don’t go anywhere else...*okay*?”

He nodded and sank back down into the balls. I knew I probably shouldn’t be leaving him alone, but it was such a pain to put his shoes back on when I was only going to be gone for a few seconds. I looked at the lady who’d glared at me. I thought about gesturing to her, asking her to keep an eye on him for me, but she still had a disapproving look on her face.

A white man with a little Latino kid...calling him Dorito?

Laci was right about something else too – I needed to learn Spanish.

I set off for the bathroom...I’d only be gone for a few seconds.

I took the time to wash my hands, but not to dry them, and I was still shaking them off and wiping them on my shirt when I got back to the play yard. I looked into the ball pit.

It was empty.

I walked over to the black netting of the ball pit and looked in, watching the balls for movement, thinking he was hiding underneath them.

“Dorito?”

Nothing.

“Dorito?” I called more loudly.

I knew he wasn’t in the ball pit. Even if he’d been trying to hide from me he never would have been able to stop himself from giggling for that long and I would have seen the balls moving by now.

“Dorito?” I called, walking around to the side of the colorful maze of tubes and tunnels. I looked up, but couldn’t see anything.

“Dorito!” I hollered up into the maze, trying to sound angry and not scared. “You come out here right now!”

A little girl, about seven, popped out of the end of the tornado slide.

"Did you see a little boy up there?" I asked her. "The one who was playing in the ball pit?"

She looked at me like I was from Mars.

Spanish.

I glanced around the play yard. It was surrounded by a high, wrought iron fence...designed to keep the kids safe from the traffic that was zooming by on the other side. The only gate was secured with a chain and padlock. If he wasn't in the play yard (which I was pretty sure by now he wasn't) he must have left by the door that went into the restaurant.

Or someone had taken him through it.

I started to panic...*really* panic. I raced over to the fence and pressed my face to it, trying to see into the parking lot. I was thinking that if someone had him, maybe they were still putting him into their car and I could get a license plate number...

"DORITO?" I hollered. "*DORITO?*"

I ran to the other side of the play yard and did the same thing because the parking lot was on both sides of the building. I couldn't see him anywhere.

I glanced up again, hoping desperately to catch a glimpse of his face peering at me through the Plexiglas window of the plastic helicopter that was on top of the maze. My pulse was pounding in my ears.

I'd only been this scared one time before...when Kyle had brought a gun to our school and we'd gone on lockdown. For hours I'd huddled in the cafeteria kitchen with a mass of other students, praying to God...*begging* Him to take care of Greg and his dad.

I started begging God now to *please* help me find Dorito...for him to suddenly appear at the end of the tornado slide.

Surprise!

At the same time, however, my mind was racing...

I'm never going to get to teach him to play soccer...I'm never going to teach him to swim...I'm never going to find him...I'll never know what's happened to him...I'll never find out...I'm going to spend the rest of my life wondering where he is...

A lady (the same one who had been glaring at me earlier) walked over to me. She started speaking to me in Spanish.

"*Está adentro*" she said. "*Te siguió a los baños*."

I didn't know what she was saying, but she was pointing into the restaurant and I knew she'd seen where he'd gone.

"Where is he? What happened to him?"

"*Ven aquí*," she said, gesturing for me to follow her. We went inside and she started pointing toward the bathrooms.

I ran back to the bathroom I had just come from and pushed open the door. It was empty and the stall doors were open so I didn't even need to lean down to make sure he wasn't there. He wasn't. I raced back out.

The woman had reached the little hallway that led to the bathrooms.

"He's not in there!" I said, shaking my head at her, my voice quavering.

"*No, no*," she said, smiling. "*Está en ese*."

She pointed at the door to the *Women's* bathroom.

I'm pretty sure she was about to go in there and get Dorito for me, but I wasn't thinking too clearly by this point and I pushed the door open and dashed inside. A middle-aged woman was standing at the hand drier and I got yet another glare of disapproval. Dorito was pressed against the sink, trying to reach the faucet.

"Dorito!" I said, dropping down onto my knees next to him. I wrapped my arms tight around his little body and held him against me. I felt absolutely sick to my stomach.

"I can't wash my hands," he said. The lady at the hand drier left.

"You were supposed to stay in the ball pit," I said, still holding him, my voice trembling.

"I had to go to the bathroom..."

"I told you to stay in the ball pit..."

"Will you help me wash my hands?"

I kept hugging him for a minute and then finally I stood up, keeping one hand on his shoulder. I reached for the faucet and turned the water on for him. He wet his hands and then stuck them under the soap dispenser, waiting for me to pump soap into them. I pushed the button two times.

"Why are you shaking?" he asked me.

"I'm not," I said.

"Yes you are..."

"It's cold in here, Dorito. It must be about fifty degrees."

"Oh."

"Did you know that this is the ladies bathroom?" I asked him as he scrubbed his hands.

"It is?"

"Uh-huh."

He smiled up at me, rinsing the soap from his hands.

"I'm not a *lady*!"

"I know you're not..." I said, shutting off the water.

"I'm a man...right?" he asked, wiping his hands off on his shirt.

"Right."

"Can I play in the ball pit some more?"

"Five more minutes," I said, catching the back of his shirt because he was trying to tear out the door in front of me.

I picked him up.

"I wanna walk!" he protested.

"You should have thought about that before you ran in here without your shoes on."

Dorito could make most of his letters all by himself in the fall. That's when Laci got pregnant for the fourth and final time.

It was November when she lost that baby.

Neither one of us was surprised. We probably would have been more surprised if she *hadn't* of lost it. We found out at her first check-up when Dr. Santos couldn't find a heartbeat on the sonogram. Laci wasn't spotting or bleeding, so they scheduled a D&C, in which they would remove the baby. It was just like an abortion, except that the baby was already dead before they started.

Two weeks after the D&C I went with Laci to one of her follow-up appointments. I sat, quietly staring out the window and not really listening, as she and Dr. Santos talked back and forth in Spanish. Suddenly the tone of Laci's voice changed and I tuned in, watching as the concern grew on her face.

"What?" I asked.

She looked at me hesitantly.

"*What?*" I demanded.

"Um..." she began. "This pregnancy was what they call a molar pregnancy."

"A molar pregnancy," I repeated and she nodded. "So what's that mean?"

"Usually nothing," she said. "That's why I didn't say anything to you earlier..."

"Usually nothing?"

She nodded.

"*But...?*"

"But there's some hormone level that's supposed to go *down* after the D&C and mine's been going *up* and...that's an indication that..."

"What, Laci?"

She hesitated.

"Tell me," I insisted. "What?"

"Apparently they can sometimes be cancerous..."

"Cancerous..."

She nodded at me.

"Are you telling me that this one was?"

She nodded again.

You have got *to be kidding me.*

Okay...to be honest, *kidding* may not have been the word that was in my mind.

"It's not a big deal," she said, reaching for my hand. I drew it away from her.

"*NOT A BIG DEAL?*" I shouted. "Are you *crazy*, Laci? You're sitting here telling me...what? That you've got *cancer*? And that's not a big deal?!"

Dr. Santos started talking; Laci listened intently.

"He says it's usually not a problem. They'll do some chemo and I'll be fine. They do it right across the street at the hospital in the outpatient clinic."

"No way, Laci!" I yelled. "We're going *HOME*! We're not staying here and letting them play around with you and then find out later that they didn't know what they were doing!"

"They aren't '*playing around*'!" Laci yelled back, looking offended that I would even suggest such a thing. "They know what they're doing. I'll be fine!"

I looked at Dr. Santos and tried to control my voice.

"I want her records sent to Dr. Sedevick," I said, reaching for my wallet. He looked at me blankly. I pulled out Dr. Sedevick's card and slapped it down on his desk in front of him.

"Send–her–records–*here*," I said to him, very slowly and loudly, tapping my finger on the card.

"Talking to him like he's an *idiot* isn't going to make him understand English," Laci said.

"Tell him then, Laci," I said, glaring at her. "Tell him to send your records home."

"NO!" she said. "This *is* home! I want to stay here. They can do everything I need right here and I can keep on working..."

"You do it NOW, Laci!" I yelled. "I mean it. We're going home and he needs to send all of your records to Dr. Sedevick...RIGHT NOW! You tell him...NOW!"

I had never yelled at her like that before...*ever*. She looked hurt and scared. In a quiet voice she spoke to Dr. Santos and pointed out the fax number on the card with a shaky finger.

In the parking lot I flipped open my cell phone.

"Who are you calling?" she asked.

"Your mom," I said. "I'm telling her what's going on and that we're coming home."

"I don't want to go," she said again in a quiet voice.

"Tough," I answered as I unlocked the car. Her mom didn't answer and I didn't leave a message.

We rode in silence until we got home. I turned off the car.

"What if I refuse to go?" she asked.

"Where are you going to live?"

"What do you mean?"

"I'm selling the house," I said.

"You can't do that!" she cried. "This is our home!"

"I *can* do it!" I told her. I was feeling more angry than I'd ever felt in my entire life and I was about to take it all out on her.

"It's *my* house...*I* pay for it and it's in *my* name. Get in there and pack up what you want. *NOW!*"

I opened my car door and stepped out, leaning back in to look at her.

"We're going *HOME!"* I shouted before I slammed the door and stormed into the house.

Two days later we were at the airport with our one-way tickets back to the United States. I had given Aaron the keys to the house and told him that they could keep using it for a while. I hadn't had any time to put it on the market anyway and I was going to have to hire someone to get in there and pack up all of the stuff that wasn't already in our suitcases. I showed him which key was the one to my office in case I needed him to send me something that I hadn't packed. I locked the office door and asked him to please keep all the kids out of it.

Laci and I had barely spoken since I'd yelled at her in the driveway. We got on the plane in silence and she wouldn't even let me help her put her carry-on luggage in the overhead rack. We sat quietly, waiting for the plane to take off. I pretended to be engrossed in the magazine someone had left stowed in the seat in front of me and I ignored the tears that I knew were streaming down her face.

It wasn't until we were taxiing down the runway that I realized I hadn't even said goodbye to Dorito.

We stayed in Jessica and Chris's basement again. My plan was that we'd stay with them for about two months until Laci's chemo was over...then we'd start looking for a place of our own.

On our first night there we both slept restlessly and Laci got up before I did the next morning. Dr. Sedevick wasn't going to be able to see us until the next day, so Jessica was going to take Laci shopping to get the apartment set back up.

I heard them upstairs, getting C.J. and Cassidy ready for preschool, and then I heard the garage door open and close as they left. When I was sure they were gone, I went upstairs.

It was cold outside – a high of twenty-eight degrees was forecast for the day, but the wind was not blowing so it wasn't too bad. I should have been downstairs setting up my office, but I felt trapped in the house and found myself drawn outside into the cold, fresh air that I hadn't felt for so long.

I was sitting in a lawn chair on the back deck, idly lining up sunflower seeds from the birdfeeder and flicking them toward a pine tree in the back lawn. That's when Mike suddenly appeared from the side yard.

He was supposed to be in medical school in Rochester, Minnesota...four hours away. The first words out of a normal friend's mouth would have been:

Wow...Mike! I'm really surprised to see you!

Or...*What are you doing here?*

Or...*I'm so glad to see you, but you really didn't need to come all this way...*

Instead, I just shook my head at him and then looked away.

"This *cannot* be happening, Mike," I finally said.

He climbed up the steps and sat down next to me. He didn't say anything.

"I can't lose her..." I said quietly, still staring into the backyard.

"You aren't going to lose her."

"You don't know that."

"Yes, I do," he said. "I can almost guarantee it."

I glanced at him, then away again.

"Listen," he said. "This thing's got almost a one hundred percent cure rate if it hasn't spread."

I didn't look back at him, but I nodded. I'd already been online and found out everything I could about molar pregnancies.

Another thing I'd learned was that Laci's particular type of pregnancy had developed only from paternal cells.

Paternal...

The father...

Me.

"Even if it *has* spread," he was saying, "you're still looking at a ninety to ninety-five percent chance that she's going to completely beat this thing."

I knew that too, but it felt really good to hear it coming out of his mouth. I finally looked back at him and was surprised to see concern etched in his face.

"If everything's gonna turn out so great," I asked him, "how come you look so worried?"

"I'm not worried about *her...*" he said, smiling slightly.

"Oh."

I hadn't handled Greg's death very well. I think everyone who loved me had spent the first year after Greg and his dad had died just waiting to find my body next to a suicide note.

"You think I'm going to have a psychotic breakdown or something?" I asked.

"Are you?"

I thought I'd dealt with Gabby's death and the miscarriages pretty well so I said, "I don't think so."

I *was* thinking, however, that at the rate things were going I was quickly becoming an expert at handling tragedies.

We sat quietly for a few moments.

"Has God ever talked to you?" Mike finally asked. "I mean, like *clearly* talked to you?"

That question shook me.

"Just one time," I finally answered. I paused for a moment. "You wanna know when?"

"When?"

"A few weeks after we'd lost Gabby. I was sitting right in there," I said, jabbing my finger toward the house, "I was looking at a paper, and I saw this ad in there for Adoption Alternatives. Have you ever heard of them?"

He nodded.

"I really wasn't even paying that much attention to it and all of a sudden God told me to call them. It was just...I don't know, it was just *overwhelming*. I'd never had Him speak to me like that before. It was amazing and I couldn't wait to tell Laci, but..."

"But, what?" Mike asked when I hesitated and shook my head.

"I didn't tell her right and she thought I was all excited about *adopting* and she didn't want to adopt and she got so upset with me that I just shut up and..."

I shrugged my shoulders.

"You never told her that God told you to call them?"

I shook my head and I didn't say anything else. It didn't take a rocket scientist to figure out that if I'd obeyed God and called the adoption agency that we would have adopted. Laci wouldn't have had two miscarriages and then a molar pregnancy. She wouldn't be facing weeks of chemo. No sense in discussing the fact that none of this would've happened if it weren't for me.

Probably Mike knew that Laci's pregnancy had developed only from *paternal* cells too...

"You wanna go in where it's warm?" I finally asked him. He looked grateful and nodded. I picked up two pieces of firewood on the way in.

We walked to the living room and Mike sat down on the couch while I opened up the wood stove. I used one of the logs to poke at the remnants that were inside before throwing them both in. I stood next to the stove for a minute and rubbed my hands over the heat. Finally I sat down on the other end of the couch.

"If you want to talk," Mike said quietly, "I'm here."

I nodded, but stayed silent for a long time. I actually wouldn't have minded talking, but it was going to be really difficult to explain to another person how I was feeling.

I liked to think that I was *way* beyond questioning why God would allow these things to happen. I'd seen first-hand how everything works to the good of those who love God. Something miraculous and eternal had resulted from Greg's death and I may not have understood yet why Gabby had died, but that didn't stop me from having faith that God would work that for good too.

"I know I fall short, Mike," I finally said. "I know that I'm not without sin...that I'm not perfect..."

I glanced up at him, trying to decide whether or not to go on. His face looked so understanding that I decided I would.

"But I think I'm a pretty good guy...you know?"

"I do too," Mike nodded.

"I mean, I'm not talking about the fact that I've been *living* in Mexico and that Laci and I have given every moment we have to helping those kids...or about how I would move *into* the landfill if God told me to do that for some reason..."

I paused for a moment.

"I'm talking about how I try to put Him first in *everything* and how I know that my relationship with Him is the most important thing and I just think...I think I do a pretty good job with that, you know, considering everything..."

Mike nodded again.

"And I don't have some misguided notion that I'm going to be spared any problems just because of my relationship with God...I know that's not how it works, but..."

I knew in my *head* that God would never leave me or forsake me, but I didn't know it in my heart. I knew He was still there, but I didn't *feel* that He was still there.

I'd prayed and prayed about it and asked Him to *please* show me that He still loved me.

Nothing but silence.

And every day I was growing more and more discouraged.

I really didn't know how to say all of this to Mike, so I didn't say anything. That's why I was very surprised when he quietly finished my sentence for me.

"But you want God to let you know that He loves you..."

A chill actually ran through my bones. It was as if Mike had read my mind and I stared at him dumbly for a moment. I could suddenly feel my pulse pounding in my throat.

"How'd you know that?" I managed to ask, swallowing hard.

"Is that right?"

"How'd you know that?" I asked again.

Mike was silent for a minute, but finally he answered.

"I've heard God speak to me clearly – like you did – only *one* time, too. *One time*. You know when that was?"

I shook my head and stared blankly at him. I had no clue.

"*Yesterday...*"

I didn't say anything.

"He told me to come here," Mike explained, "you know...to talk to you."

I kept staring at him.

"Don't you get it?" Mike finally asked.

I shook my head slowly.

"He told me to come here and talk to you," Mike said again. "He wanted me to tell you that He loves you."

A few hours later Jessica and Laci got home. They were both surprised to find Mike there and I could tell that Laci was really glad to see him. We went out to the car and helped carry packages down to the basement. Laci made it a point to talk to Mike and Jessica, but not to me. I didn't really blame her.

When we were done putting the packages away, Jessica offered to make everybody some lunch and Mike went with her upstairs. Laci tried to follow, but I caught her arm.

"We need to talk," I said.

She shook her arm free.

"Not now," she said in a low voice. "We have company."

"Please, Laci," I said. "Please..."

She softened, but just a little.

"Hurry up."

"Come here," I said, taking her hand and leading her to the couch. I sat and tugged her down next to me. "Sit down."

"What?" she said, reluctantly sitting beside me. If I hadn't still been holding her hand I think she would have crossed her arms at me.

"I'm so sorry, Laci," I began. "I love you more than anything in this world. I'm so sorry."

Her eyes filled with tears and I knew she was going to forgive me so I kissed her.

"I shouldn't have made you leave Mexico and I never should have talked to you the way I did," I continued. "You *have* to know that I didn't mean what I said about the house..."

She looked at me and blinked. Tears fell onto her cheeks.

"I don't really feel that way," I promised her. "*Please* don't think I meant what I said. We're not going to sell the house. As soon as your treatments are through we'll go right back down there to our house...*our* house. I don't know why I even said what I did. I didn't mean it at all."

"You were scared," she said quietly.

"I *was* scared," I admitted, "but mostly I was mad...but it doesn't matter. I shouldn't have said what I did at all – no matter *how* I felt. Can you forgive me?"

"You were mad?"

"Can you forgive me?" I asked her again.

"I forgive you," she said, laying one hand on my cheek and kissing me. "What do you mean you were mad?"

"I was mad at myself."

"What are you talking about?" she asked.

I paused for a moment before going on.

"You know how God talks to you sometimes?" I asked her. She nodded.

"Well," I said, "He doesn't do that to me. He usually just leads me, or guides me. It's...it's different. You know?"

"He does that to me, too," she said, nodding.

"But He *has* talked to you, right?"

"Just about really important stuff," she said, smiling, and I knew she was referring to the times when God had told her that we were supposed to be with each other.

"Well," I said, hesitating. "He's only talked to me like that one time...just *once*."

"When?"

I paused.

"Remember after Gabby died?" I finally said. "When you were packing to go back to Mexico and I came down here with that ad for Adoption Alternatives?"

She nodded at me, looking confused.

"God told me to call them..."

I let *that* hang in the air for a minute.

"He told you to call them?" she finally repeated.

I nodded.

"And you didn't," she said slowly, "because I got so upset..."

"I should have called them no matter what you said or did," I replied. "He told me to do something and I didn't do it."

"You don't think *this* is your fault, do you?" she asked, putting her hand on her belly.

It sure didn't take her long to make that leap.

"I think there are definite consequences for our actions," I said.

"I do too," she agreed, "but even if we'd called the adoption agency *that very day...*even if they'd found us a baby....I still would have wanted my own baby too. I *still* would have tried to have one and all this still would have happened..."

"Maybe," I said. "All I know is that I've felt very cut off from God ever since then and if He ever does trust me enough to speak to me again, I'm definitely going to do what He tells me to do...no matter what."

"What do you mean...you've '*felt cut off from God*'?"

"I mean He hasn't let me know that He's been there at all. He hasn't let me know that He loves me, or that He cares about me...*nothing*. He's just been silent."

"I cannot believe you haven't told me any of this!" she said. "All this time you've felt like God doesn't love you and you're just now telling me?"

"Well, I *knew* He loved me in my mind...I just...oh, I don't know," I said. "I can't explain it...that's probably why I didn't tell you. Plus, I think I kept hoping it would get better."

"Did it?" she asked quietly.

I nodded and smiled.

"Mike?" she guessed.

I nodded again.

"I'm glad," she said. "But David! You have *got* to talk to me! How am I supposed to know how to pray for you when I don't even know what's going on?"

She sounded mad.

"I'm sorry?" I tried.

"I can't believe you never told me any of this," she said, shaking her head.

"Look," I said. "I can't help it if I'm not all open with my feelings like you are. You knew what you were getting into when you married me."

"Like I had a choice!" she said, rolling her eyes and then she smiled at me. "I don't know why God couldn't have decided to hook me up with a good looking doctor or something."

“Oh,” I moaned. “Please don’t tell me that you use to have a thing for Mike, too!?”

“Naw,” she said, smiling. “But I bet I could’ve had him if I’d wanted him!”

“You could have had anybody you wanted,” I agreed.

I woke Mike up in the middle of the night. He was sleeping on Jessica and Christopher's couch in the living room because he'd offered to go with us to our first doctor's appointment tomorrow.

"Mike..."

He sat up slowly.

"What's going on?" he asked, rubbing his eyes.

"I'm really sorry to bother you," I said, "but Laci's not feeling too good..."

That perked him right up.

"What's wrong with her?"

"I don't know," I said. "Is she still supposed to be bleeding a lot?"

"Define *a lot*."

"I don't know. She says it's a lot."

"Can I go take a look at her?" he asked. He was already grabbing a small bag out of his suitcase.

I followed him down the stairs.

"Hey, Laci," he said when he saw her. She was slumped against her pillow, staring straight ahead. She didn't acknowledge that he had spoken to her.

"How're you feeling?"

He touched her forehead and then he put his fingers to her neck, feeling her pulse.

"Hey...Laci?" he said, as he pulled a blood pressure cuff out and wrapped it around her arm. "Can you tell me anything? Can you tell me how you're feeling?"

Laci didn't answer him, she just closed her eyes. Mike started pumping up the blood pressure cuff and as soon as he'd taken the reading he opened his cell phone.

"What's the address here again?" he asked me.

I had to think for a minute.

"Um...137 Buckhorn..." I said.

He nodded and punched some numbers into his cell phone.

"I need an ambulance at 137 Buckhorn..."

An ambulance?

"Female," he said. "Twenty-three years old. BP of 80 over 40. Pulse is thready...120."

Mike listened to his phone and then he continued.

"She's two weeks out from a D & C for choriocarcinoma. Heavy vaginal bleeding...probable hemorrhagic shock."

He paused for a few moments, listening. "Yes...but very shallow."

Her breathing...it *was* shallow.

"Okay," he said into his phone and then he closed it.

"What's going on, Mike?" I said.

"She's in shock from losing so much blood..."

"Is she going to be all right?"

"Sure she is," he said. Her eyes fluttered opened and she stared straight ahead again, not focused on anything.

"Hi, Laci," he said. "You're going to be fine, okay?"

He picked her up and I followed him again as he carried her upstairs and laid her on the couch in the living room. He wiped his hand across her forehead and I noticed how damp her hair was. Her arms and legs were trembling too.

Suddenly Laci's eyes rolled back into her head – just like in the movie *The Exorcist*. Now I'd never actually *seen* that movie, but whenever someone wants to describe how somebody's eyes roll back into their head they always say: "It was just like in *The Exorcist!*"

If that's really what it looked like in the movie, I knew I didn't want to see it. Then – just in case things weren't scary enough – Laci started throwing up.

"What's going on?" I turned to find Jessica standing behind me in her bathrobe. She took one look at Laci and turned white.

"She's fine," Mike insisted. "She's going to be fine."

Mike was doing a pretty good job staying calm, but I saw a look of great relief wash across his face when he heard a siren. By the time the ambulance had come to a complete stop at the curb he'd already carried Laci out the front door with me and Jessica at his heels.

The paramedics opened the back of the ambulance and pulled out a metal stretcher. Mike laid Laci down on it and started telling them her medical history. They slid her into the ambulance and Mike climbed up with her...then he stopped and looked back at me.

"Here," he said, jumping back down. "You go."

"No," I said. "Go ahead. You'll do more good than me. I'll be right behind you."

Mike didn't argue with me. He hopped back up into the ambulance and I saw him sit down next to Laci and take her hand before the doors closed and it raced off.

God hadn't just shown me that He loved me that day...He'd also put a certainty in my heart that Laci was going to be okay. I don't know how I knew this, but I did. I was also sure that Mike had been sent not just to help me, but to help Laci, too.

Mike and Laci had both done such a good job of doing whatever God had asked them to do. It only seemed fitting that they should ride to the hospital together.

About ten o'clock the next morning, Laci finally started to wake up. Her mom and dad were on one side of her bed and I was on the other. Her mother was stroking Laci's hair and telling her how lucky she was that Mike had been there last night and how glad they were that she was going to be okay.

They'd been at the hospital all night, so when Mike knocked lightly on the door and came in they thanked him again for everything he'd done and then excused themselves to go to the cafeteria for some breakfast.

"Hey, Laci," he said, smiling at her. "You're looking good. How're you feeling?"

"Tired..." she said. "Where am I?"

"She just woke up," I explained.

"Oh," Mike said. "You're at the hospital."

"What happened?" she asked.

Mike looked at me questioningly.

"You can tell her," I said. I didn't want to.

"Laci," he said, "you were hemorrhaging quite a bit last night..."

"I didn't feel good," she said, trying to remember.

"The bleeding," Mike went on, "was...*severe*."

He looked to make sure she was paying attention.

"They had to do an emergency hysterectomy to save your life...you would have died otherwise."

I was watching her to see if she understood what he was saying...no more uterus...no more pregnancies...no more babies.

"Listen," he said. "They were able to leave your ovaries..."

"Okay," she said slowly.

"That's really good, Laci," he continued.

"Why?" she asked. I could tell she was still trying to process everything he was saying.

"Several reasons," he said. "You won't have to go through menopause right now and you still have eggs...if you ever want to look into having a surrogate carry your biological children, you'll probably be able to do that..."

"Ohhhhhh," she moaned, her hand sliding down toward her belly. "It hurts."

"Here," he said, reaching for a little button on a cord that was attached to a machine on the other side of her bed. "Morphine. Greatest thing ever invented. All you gotta do is push this button..."

He showed her how to depress the button and within a few seconds I could see relief spread across her face. In less than two minutes she'd drifted off to sleep again and he draped the cord over her bed rail so she'd be able to reach it.

When she woke back up Mike was gone. He had a long drive ahead of him and I'd insisted that he go ahead and leave.

"Where's Mike?" she asked.

"I made him go on."

"Oh," she said, closing her eyes again. "I wanted to say thank you..."

"He knows," I said. "Laci?"

"Hmmm?" She opened her eyes.

"Do you...did you understand what Mike was telling you?"

She nodded.

"I'm really sorry, Laci," I said, stroking her hair.

"It should be easy to have kids," she said.

"You mean that surrogate thing?" I asked, surprised.

"No," she said, smiling slightly and shaking her head. "I work at an orphanage."

"Oh," I said, smiling back. "I love you."

"I love you, too," she said, and then she gasped, "Ow."

She reached for the cord that Mike had draped over her rail and pushed the button.

Dr. Sedivick referred us to an oncologist named Dr. Owens. He was very business-like and never smiled, but at least he spoke English and I understood everything that he said.

"Since your uterus has been removed the chances that the cancer has metastasized is minimal. Your lungs look clear and that's good...it often shows up there first if it's spread. I'd like to schedule you for six weeks of chemo and after that you'll report back for check-ups once every three months for the first year...every six months for two years after that...and then once a year for two more years. Do you have any questions?"

Laci shook her head.

"I do," I said. "We're going back to Mexico after her treatments are over. Do we need to come back here for her follow-up appointments? I mean, if we do that's fine...I was just wondering."

"What part of Mexico?"

"Mexico City..."

"I think I can make arrangements for you to have most of the follow-ups there. I have a colleague here who's fluent in Spanish...he can be a go-between for us and that way I can still be your primary physician and talk to you whenever you have questions if you'd like."

I nodded.

"When do we start?" Laci asked.

"You're healing well, but let's wait a few days to give your body a little rest." He jotted something down on a piece of paper. "Take this to the front desk and they'll schedule your first treatment."

The night before her first chemo appointment, I was lying in bed, trying unsuccessfully to get to sleep. Laci had her head on my chest and I could tell by the way she was breathing that she wasn't asleep either.

"Are you okay?" I asked, kissing the top of her head.

I felt her shrug.

"What's wrong, Laci? Are you scared?"

She nodded.

"I'm sorry," I said, hugging her tight.

"I don't want to lose my hair," she said and I could feel her tears on my chest. "I know I shouldn't care about that...but I do. I don't want to lose my hair."

"Laci," I said, surprised. "You're not going to lose your hair!"

"How do you know?" she asked.

"Honestly," I said. "Don't you *ever* go online?"

She turned on the light and looked at me.

After we'd gotten home from Dr. Owens' office I'd looked at our copy of the chemo orders and had typed in the names of each of the drugs that she was going to be given.

Some tiredness...general weakness...nausea.

Not a picnic, but nowhere near what it could have been.

"Are you serious?" she asked. "I'm not going to lose my hair?"

"I don't think so," I said.

She grinned at me.

"I can't believe you were worried about that, anyway," I said. "It wouldn't matter if you lost your hair."

"You love my hair," she argued.

"No," I said. "I love *you*."

Chemo was a snap (well, at least it was for me – and Laci kept insisting that it wasn't too bad so I decided to believe her). About four weeks into her treatments I caught her tugging on her hair. She smiled at me when she saw me looking at her in the mirror.

"I told you so," I said.

Christmas came...our third one together. Our last Christmas had not been a particularly happy time for us – Laci had just had her first miscarriage. This Christmas the mood was *so* much better.

I had absolutely no idea what to get Laci though and finally I had to just ask her.

"What are we going to get each other for Christmas?"

"I don't know," she shrugged. "I already got you something."

Great.

"Come on, Laci. You're so impossible."

"I liked what you did the last two years," she said, smiling.

"If I could I'd do it again," I said, "but I can't so you're going to have to give me some ideas."

"Why can't you do it again?"

"Hello?!" I said, waving my hand in front of her face. "Have you looked outside lately? The ground is covered with snow. We're not in Mexico anymore, Toto."

"You could still do it," she laughed.

"You want me to buy a hundred and twenty gifts and mail them down there before Christmas?"

"No, silly. Just have Aaron do it and pay him back."

"Are you serious?" I asked her. "That would make you happy even if you couldn't be there to hand them out?"

"That would make me *very* happy," she said.

I could tell she was serious so I told her okay and then I called Aaron. I also managed to figure out something to buy so she'd have something to unwrap on Christmas morning.

Finally I called Aaron one more time and I told him to watch for an express mail package from the States.

For our Christmas present my parents threw a Christmas Eve party for us and *everybody* was there. It was pretty much everyone who'd been at our rehearsal dinner...everybody that we loved.

Even Mike was there and Natalie was home for the holidays.

"That 'in sickness and in health' thing kinda hit you guys fast, didn't it?" Tanner asked me.

"Tell me about it."

"Mike says she's pretty much in the clear though?"

"Yeah," I nodded. "She's going to be fine. She can't wait to get back to Mexico and start adopting kids."

"When are you going back?"

"Well, she's got one more week of treatments and then we want to be here for her one-month follow-up appointment, but we'll probably go back right after that."

"So you're going to be here for at least another month?"

"Why do I get the feeling you're about to hit me up for a favor?"

"Who? *Me*?"

"Whatdya want?"

"If Jordan doesn't get a letter from his math teacher in February saying that he's making at least a "C", he's not going to get to try out for baseball."

"I'd *love* to help Jordan in math," I said, smiling.

"That's what I figured."

For Christmas Laci gave me an envelope. I was impressed when I read what was inside for two reasons. First of all, it indicated that she had reserved a room for us at the same ski lodge our youth group had gone to in the seventh grade. I'd loved that place and had always wanted to go back. Secondly, she'd made the reservations *online*...I was looking at the printout from the computer.

"Who helped you do this?" I asked suspiciously.

"I did it all by myself," she insisted. "It's not that hard really..."

"That's what I've been telling you all along," I said, throwing my hands up in the air.

Then I slid four packages toward her and she looked worried.

"You still did the thing at the orphanage, right?" she asked.

"Yes, I still did the thing at the orphanage."

"Okay, good!" she smiled, taking the presents.

The big one was a manger and the little ones were Mary and Joseph and baby Jesus.

"They're made by Fontanini," I told her. "They make a whole line of these...you can keep adding things every year...shepherds and wise men and stuff."

"Oh," she said. "That'll be great!"

"You don't have a clue why I gave you this, do you?"

She looked at me blankly.

"They're unbreakable..." I said, picking up Joseph and whacking him a few times on the coffee table.

"Don't do that to Jesus' father!" Laci cried.

"Joseph isn't His father."

"You *know* what I mean," she said, snatching him from me. "You don't need to beat him on the table."

"Don't you get it, Laci? I bought them so our kids can set up the manger every year and look at it and touch it and stuff and we won't need to worry about it getting broken."

When I was little my mom and dad had always yelled at me to leave our manger alone and you could see the line around Mary's neck where my mom had glued her head back on.

"Oh," Laci said. She looked really happy now. "That was a great idea. I love it!"

"I have another surprise for you, too."

"Another one?" she asked.

I nodded.

"What?"

"*Estoy aprendiendo hablar español.*"

Her eyes got really wide and her mouth dropped open.

"Did I say that right?"

"You're learning to speak Spanish?" she asked slowly.

"Yup! I mean *si Señora.*"

"*¿Cuando empezó hablar español?*"

I think she asked me when I'd started learning it.

Ever since I thought Dorito had been kidnapped from McDonald's.

"*Hacen unos cuantos meses*," I answered.

A couple of months ago.

Her eyes got wide again and she smiled.

"*No puedo creer que estas aprendiendo español. ¡Esto es tan fantástico! ¿Como lo has estado aprendiendo? ¿Has estado escuchando las cintas que te di? ¿Están buenos? ¿Cuanto sabes?*"

"Whoa! Whoa! Whoa!" I said. "Too much! Too much! *Todavía no soy tan bueno con el español.*"

I'm not very good at Spanish yet.

"*Lo serás*," she said, smiling broadly.

You will be.

"Uncle Dave....Aunt Laci?" Cassidy yelled from the top of the stairs.

"What?"

"Are you guys coming up here? Mommy says we can't open anything until you come up here."

"*Ahora vamos*," Laci called back, laughing.

"What?" Cassidy asked.

"She said we'll be right there!" I hollered. Then I looked at her uncertainly. "Right?"

Laci nodded at me and laughed again. "*Cierto*."

We went upstairs and watched Cassidy and CJ tear into their presents and when Jessica pulled caramel rolls out of the oven we all tore into those.

After we were done, Laci called the orphanage.

"*Inez, es Laci. ¿Han abierto los regalos los niños?*"

I think she asked if the kids had opened their presents yet.

She babbled on in Spanish for a little while and I could tell enough from the words I understood and by the look on her face that the kids had opened their presents and liked everything. After a few minutes she held the phone out to me.

"Merry Christmas, Inez!" I said.

"Day-Day!"

"Oh! Dorito!" I said and Laci smiled at me. I smiled back. "How are you doing?"

"I'm a good boy."

"I know you are," I said. "*How* are you doing?"

"I'm doing good."

"Well, good!" I said. "Merry Christmas!"

"Merry Christmas, Day-Day! Guess what?"

"What?"

"Santa gave me The Count!"

"Are you *serious*?" I asked, trying to sound very, very surprised.

"Uh-huh."

"I wonder how he knew that you liked The Count?"

"I don't know," Dorito said and I could hear the awe in his voice.

"I can't wait to see him!"

"Where are you?" Dorito asked.

"I'm in Cavendish...remember all those pictures in my office that I showed you with the snow?"

"Yeah..."

"That's where I am. I'm with the snow."

"Are you coming back?"

"Of course I am!"

"When?"

"Laci hasn't been feeling very good and as soon as she gets all better we'll come home, okay?"

"Okay."

"I miss you."

"Bye, Day-Day."

"Bye, Dorito."

Inez came back on the phone.

"Merry Christmas, Señor David," she said in her thick accent.

"Merry Christmas, Inez. He sounds good. He hasn't forgotten any of his English!"

"No, no Señor David. We practice everyday."

"How are his legs?"

"They're good, but someone called and said he needs new braces again on his legs. They said you already had an appointment made for him next week but I don't know anything about it..."

"Oh...I did. I forgot all about it. He's got an appointment on the second. Can you make sure he goes to it?"

"I don't know, Señor David..."

"Please, Inez? They've got all my billing information and everything...he's just going to need this one last set..."

She hesitated for a moment but then finally said she'd make sure he got there.

"Thanks, Inez," I said, breathing a sigh of relief.

"Merry Christmas, Señor David."

"Merry Christmas."

Jordan came over the day after Christmas so I could start tutoring him.

"Hi, Jordan," Jessica greeted him as she opened the door (Jessica used to babysit him and his middle brother Chase when they were little).

"Hi, Jess," he said as I came out of the kitchen with a brownie. "Hi David."

"Hi, Jordan. You want a brownie?"

"Okay."

I went back into the kitchen and put one on a napkin for him and grabbed another one for myself for good measure.

"Come on," I said, opening the door to the basement. "It'll be quieter down here."

We sat down at my work table.

"Where's your textbook?" I asked him.

"We had to turn them in at the end of the semester," he explained. "We're on block schedule."

"So you just finished a math class?"

"Yeah."

"What was it?"

"Prealgebra."

"Okay, great. What are you taking this next semester?"

"Prealgebra," he said quietly.

"You flunked it?"

"Yeah," he sighed. "I always flunk math."

"Not anymore."

He looked at me doubtfully.

"Look," I whispered. "I got *Laci* through math. If I can get *Laci* through math I can get *anybody* through math. Okay?"

He smiled at me. "Okay."

Laci had her last round of chemo just before New Year's and we went skiing right after that. She was kind of down and out on the second and third day from her treatments, but we were there for five days.

"You think you're going to hit the slopes today?" I asked her on the fourth day.

"Maybe this afternoon," she said. "I'm ruining our vacation, aren't I?"

"No you're not," I said. "I just wish you weren't feeling so bad."

"I'm not feeling that bad. I'm just really tired."

"You always say that."

"You should have brought Jordan up here instead. You guys could've worked on math *all day*."

I smiled at her. For the last week, Jordan had been coming over to the house every day and working with me for at least two hours each time.

"What's he going to do when we go back to Mexico?" she asked.

I shook my head.

"I don't know. I'm kind of worried about him."

"Is he doing that bad?"

"I guess not...he just had a really bad year when their dad left and he got so far behind in math that he hasn't been able to catch up."

"Are you gonna be able to get him caught up before we fly home?"

"I'm gonna try."

When we got back, Laci kept busy by going out with Jessica during the week and Ashlyn on the weekends. Natalie drove in one more time from Colorado and I thought it seemed that Laci was finally happy; enjoying things and relaxing.

She had an appointment scheduled with Dr. Owens for the end of January to make sure that everything was okay, but we already both knew that it was. I bought plane tickets for the first Wednesday in February.

Fifteen days before we were to leave, a feeling began gnawing at me that we shouldn't leave Cavendish. I kept wondering if Laci was feeling the same thing too, but if she was, she didn't say anything about it.

Then, ten days before we were supposed to leave, God decided it was time to give me another try.

Call them.

What had happened before had scared me enough that I didn't want to mess around. I called them first and *then* I told Laci.

"Are you sure?" she asked.

"Pretty sure," I replied.

"*Pretty sure?*"

"Pretty sure," I nodded.

She looked exasperated.

"It doesn't make sense," she said. "Why would He want us to call them when we're getting ready to go back to the *orphanage* in Mexico? It doesn't make any sense."

"I already called them," I said.

"You did?"

"Uh-huh."

"What did they say?"

"They said: 'Hello? Adoption Alternatives. This is Janet. How may I help you?'"

"This isn't funny, David."

"We have an appointment to go down there tomorrow morning."

Chemo might have been a snap, but the whole cancer-thing had scared Laci, too.

"Okay," she sighed. "We'll go see them tomorrow."

The next day we drove to Adoption Alternatives. It was located in an old house in the restored part of town. We parked behind a car that had a little Christian fish on the bumper. The fish had sprouted feet and the word '*Darwin*' was written inside of it.

Janet ushered us into an old bedroom that was set up to look like an office and told us that the adoption counselor, Starr, would be with us soon.

We sat down and looked at the posters on the wall. A ceramic Buddha smiled at us from the desk. I could hear what sounded like a waterfall or a fountain, but I couldn't find its source.

Starr came into the office, looking all of about seventeen years of age. She was wearing a Green Peace t-shirt and cargo pants. There was a star tattooed on her neck.

Star...Starr.

Cute.

We stood up when she entered the room. She extended her hand.

"Hello, I'm Starr."

"Hi," I said, shaking her hand. 'I'm David and this is my wife, Laci."

It might have been my imagination, but I thought I saw a flash of surprise cross her face.

"You're interested in adopting?" she asked, sitting down.

Adopting? From our orphanage in Mexico? Yes! From here? No!

"Yes," Laci and I both said as we sat back down.

"How about if I go over our procedures and then you can let me know if you have any questions. Is that cool?"

Cool.

"A pregnant woman who doesn't want her baby and decides not to terminate her pregnancy can come to us to search for the person or persons that she would like to have raise her baby.

"Prospective parents fill out a lengthy questionnaire," she said, handing us a thick red folder. "The expectant mothers browse through the files until they find the parent or parents that look most attractive to them. We set up a meeting and – if things go well – our office helps to work out all the details of the adoption."

Laci opened up the folder and we looked at the top sheet. The first thing I saw was a section with eight boxes to choose from:

□Single (male) □Single (female)
□Single (other) □Couple(male/female)
□Couple (male/male) □Couple (female/female)
□Couple (other) □Other

Other?

Okay, now I was beginning to see why this place was called Adoption *Alternatives*. I was also beginning to understand one of the posters on the wall.

I took the folder from Laci and looked at it closer.

The next section asked you to describe your religious preference. I won't even get into what options were listed there.

"Are all of the adoptions open?" Laci was asking.

"Usually," Starr answered, "but not always. Sometimes the mother changes her mind and decides it will be easier not to see her baby after the adoption is complete."

"We live in Mexico," I said quickly.

"You *live* in Mexico?"

We both nodded.

And we're conservative Christians, I wanted to add, but I kept my mouth shut.

"Why did you choose our agency?" she asked carefully.

My horoscope told me to.

"We felt drawn to come here," Laci said. Starr nodded and seemed pleased with that answer.

"Is it possible that someone would choose us even though we live in Mexico?" Laci asked.

"It's possible..." Starr said.

Is it possible that any mother who wants to place their baby through your agency would actually ever pick someone like us?

"So we need to fill this out?" Laci asked.

We left the clinic with the packet and got into the car.

"What do you think?" Laci asked as we pulled away.

"You don't want to know," I answered.

"I think we need to fill this stuff out right away and get it back to them as soon as we can," Laci said.

"You don't really think someone who chooses that agency is actually going to pick *us*, do you?"

"No," Laci admitted, "but that's not our problem. I say we fill it out honestly, get it back to them, and then get on with our lives. It'll be up to God after that."

"So we're still flying back to Mexico next week?"

"Unless He tells us otherwise," she said.

"Deal," I answered.

Do you know how long it took for God to 'tell us otherwise'?

Five days.

Someone actually wanted to meet us and talk to us about adopting her baby. Some girl named Kelly. Before I knew it we were back in Starr's office, listening to the sound of a waterfall or a fountain and waiting for Kelly to arrive. We didn't look at the posters this time...we just stared at each other in disbelief.

Kelly entered the room and sat down. She didn't look very pregnant yet. She was pretty...she had long, strawberry blond hair and blue eyes. But she also had a sad, haunted look about her.

"Kelly," Starr said, "this is Laci and this is David."

Kelly nodded at us and we nodded back. Then Kelly looked down at the floor. Starr told us she was going to leave us alone so that we could get to know one another a little bit.

"How are you, Kelly?" Laci asked her as Starr pulled the door closed behind her.

Kelly looked back up at us.

"You don't remember me, do you?"

Remember you?

"Have we met?" Laci asked gently.

Kelly nodded.

"I'm Kelly Dunn," she said. "Kyle's sister."

I know my mouth dropped open.

"Kyle Dunn?" Laci asked.

Kelly nodded.

Kyle Dunn?

The Kyle Dunn who had killed my best friend and his father?

My mind flashed back to the execution.

It was. It was the same young teenage girl who'd tried to comfort her mother as they'd watched Kyle die.

I was speechless.

"I recognized your picture," she said, holding up the file we'd compiled a few days ago. "Kyle told me and my mom all about you."

"How's your mom?" Laci asked quietly.

Kelly shrugged. I rubbed my forehead.

"Why did you contact us, Kelly?" Laci asked.

"You want a baby, right?" She looked to Laci and then to me.

I managed a slight nod.

"When I saw your picture I remembered what you did for Kyle. I want the same thing for my baby."

"What's that?" Laci asked. "What exactly do you want for your baby?"

"To grow up in a home with people like you...not someone like me or my mom."

"People like us?"

"Yeah, you know...people who believe in God."

"If you don't believe in God," Laci asked, "why do you care if your baby grows up with people who do?"

"Oh," Kelly said. "I believe in God, I just meant people who're better than me."

"We're not better than you," I said.

"You know what I mean," Kelly replied. "People who go to church and stuff."

Oh, boy.

When Laci and I got back into the car we didn't say anything to each other for the entire ride home. We pulled up in the driveway. I turned off the car and finally looked over at Laci.

"Our tickets aren't refundable, are they?" she asked. I shook my head. She sighed and we got out of the car and walked inside.

We started meeting with Kelly on a regular basis to get to know her. It was so obvious right from the beginning (even to me) that God wanted us to minister to Kelly. No, actually, God wanted *Laci* to minister to Kelly.

Kelly wanted absolutely nothing to do with me.

"What'd I ever do to her?" I asked after Laci had met with her for their second lunch together without me.

"Well," Laci said, "she probably thinks you hate her because her brother killed your best friend."

"I don't hate her."

"I know you don't, but she doesn't know that."

"Why doesn't she think *you* hate her?" I asked.

"Because I'm sweet," Laci smiled. "She can tell I don't hate her."

"I'm sweet!" I argued and Laci laughed.

"That's not the word I would use to describe you when you realized who she was."

"Well, I was shocked, Laci. You've got to admit that kind of came out of nowhere."

"I know," she said. "I'm not blaming you, I'm just telling you why Kelly probably doesn't feel all that comfortable around you."

The truth was that I didn't feel all that comfortable around her either.

"I think you need to go ahead and put the house on the market..." Laci said.

"NO!" I replied, surprising myself by how adamant I sounded. "She never said that we have to stay around here..."

"We haven't talked about it," Laci said.

"We put in our file that we *live* in Mexico."

"I don't think she read our file," Laci said. "I think once she recognized our picture she didn't look any farther than that."

"That's *her* problem."

"Kelly," Laci said the next time the three of us got together. "We need to talk about something."

"Okay."

"Did you read our application?"

Kelly nodded.

"No," Laci said. "I mean did you really *read* it? Do you know that we live in Mexico?"

"You live here," Kelly said, a confused look on her face.

"Not really," Laci said. "We live in Mexico. We're just here for...for a while."

"Oh."

"Is it going to be a problem for you if we take the baby to Mexico? You won't be able to see him very often..."

"I don't know," Kelly admitted. "Can I think about it for a while?"

"Sure," Laci said.

"I just know I want you two to be its parents," Kelly said, looking at me and then at Laci.

Laci smiled at her. I just sighed.

We went with Kelly to her twelve week appointment and heard the baby's heart beat. Afterwards we took her out to eat and brought up the subject of Mexico once more.

"I don't know," Kelly told us again, looking down at her plate. "I haven't decided."

"She's just stringing us along, Laci," I complained after we'd dropped her off at her house.

"What are you talking about?"

"I mean she needs to go ahead and make a decision. Either she's okay with us taking the baby to Mexico or she's not. If she's not then she needs to start looking for somebody else."

"David, we have to take this baby no matter what!"

"Even if she doesn't want us going to Mexico?"

"Yes."

"You're serious?" I asked her. "You'd stay here and raise her baby and not go back to Mexico?"

"Yes."

"*Why?*"

"She needs us, David. Her baby needs us."

"No, Laci. There are a ton of Christian couples who would *love* to have her baby...you know that. She could just go to a Christian adoption agency. As soon as they found out she's having a white baby they'd have so many people clamoring to pay her medical bills and help her out that she wouldn't know who to pick. It doesn't have to be us."

"Yes it does."

"Why?"

"It just does, David. You know that."

I pulled over to the side of the road and put the car in park. I looked out my window.

"What's the matter?" she finally asked softly. I didn't say anything, I just shook my head.

"You've got to talk to me," she said, putting her hand on my shoulder.

"I don't want this baby," I finally said, still staring out my window.

"I know," she said softly.

I looked at her.

"Do *you* want this baby?"

"No."

"Then what are we doing, Laci?"

"We're obeying God."

"I can't believe He wants us raising a child we don't want."

"We'll want it by the time it's ours," she said. "I know we will. We'll love it."

"I just can't see it happening," I said, shaking my head.

"There was a time when I couldn't see myself ever loving you," she said, "but I do. I love you with all my heart."

"This is different."

"How? How is it different?"

"This baby will always be related to Kyle...*always*. Every time I look at him or her I'm going to remember that."

"We've forgiven Kyle..."

"But we haven't forgotten what he did," I said, feeling tears in my eyes. "I don't want to spend the rest of my life thinking about that every time I see my child."

"You won't," she assured me. "I promise you that God will let you love this child and not think about that."

"I don't know, Laci."

"What about women who get pregnant because they've been raped? You've heard stories about them being able to raise their babies and love them in spite of how they were conceived."

"Most of them put their babies up for adoption because they don't want to be reminded about it every day," I said, not sure if that was actually true or not.

"But not *all* of them," she argued back. "I've heard some of them on talk shows and stuff talking about raising their babies and about how much they love them..."

I shook my head and looked back out the window.

"She's having a sonogram in two weeks," Laci went on. "Maybe after we see the baby...maybe we'll start to feel differently then."

I leaned my head against the headrest and closed my eyes. Laci let me sit there for a minute.

"I guess I don't have much choice," I finally said.

"You can choose if you're going to have faith in God or not."

"That's not fair, Laci. If I didn't have faith I wouldn't be going through with this. You know that."

"Well," she said, "you can choose what your *attitude* about it's going to be."

She had me there.

"Okay," I finally nodded and I started the car and drove home.

We started praying that God would put a love in our hearts for Kelly's baby. Of course we already had a certain kind of love for her baby just because it was one of God's children, but we wanted to feel about it the way we'd felt about Gabby...or at least close.

I tried to have a better attitude...to give thanks even though I didn't feel particularly thankful.

It helped a lot that Laci was struggling with the same thing. Somehow I didn't feel like such a louse.

When Kelly was sixteen weeks pregnant we went with her to her sonogram. I was hoping that as soon as I saw the baby on the screen I would feel something for it, but I didn't. When I wasn't thinking about Gabby I was thinking about Kyle. I barely blinked when the technician told us it was a boy.

We took her out after that appointment too and brought up the subject of Mexico once more. This time she'd made a decision.

"I can't raise him myself...I know that," she said, "but I love him and I still want to be a part of his life."

She also told us she wanted us to think of a name for him. She thought it should be our decision, but she wanted to know as soon as possible. She said she'd read somewhere that she should be talking to the baby and she thought it would be good if she started calling him by his name.

When we'd been expecting Gabby, we'd spent a lot of time picking out baby names and arguing until we'd found the right one. Laci had wanted a Spanish name and of course I hadn't. We'd finally compromised, deciding to name her Gabrielle and call her Gabby.

But before we'd known that Gabby was going to be a girl, I had sometimes wondered – if the baby was a boy – if we might name it Greg.

I'd wondered then if that would be too weird. Would it be appropriate? I'd never brought it up and then we'd found out we were having a girl, so it hadn't mattered anyway.

Now, however, we knew we were having a boy. What about now? Would it be too weird now?

Hi, baby. Your name is Greg. We named you after my best friend...you know...the one who was killed by your uncle?

No. That didn't seem weird at all.

We settled on Stephen.

Kelly didn't understand at first why we'd decided to call the baby Stephen. Then Laci read to her from Acts and explained Stephen's story. When Laci got to the part about how the last thing Stephen had done was to ask God's forgiveness for the people who were killing him, Kelly finally understood.

We still hadn't picked out a middle name though.

After rereading Acts, Laci asked me if it could be Paul. I knew why she wanted that for his middle name and she was right...it would have been perfect.

But I said no.

I just couldn't do it...

That's what Greg's dad's name had been and what the "P" had stood for in Gregory P. White.

Resigned to the fact that we were in Cavendish to stay, we started getting involved again with the community we'd grown up in. Laci rejoined the church choir and we started going to the adult Bible study on Tuesday nights. I went to the high school baseball team's games to cheer Jordan on in the spring and he finished out the school year with a "B" in Pre-algebra.

Summer came and Laci and I joined the pool. I quickly discovered that the pool's not all that much fun if you're not a teenager and you're not hanging out with your friends all day long.

I did start working out though and one day I timed myself in the events I'd competed in during high school and college. I was mortified by my times...they were abysmal.

"You haven't trained in over three years," Laci said when I complained to her. "What'd you expect?"

I hadn't expected to feel so old when I was only in my mid-twenties.

"Just keep working out this summer," Laci told me, "and then join the YMCA in the fall."

But I didn't want to join the YMCA in the fall...I didn't want to even *be* here in the fall...I wanted to be back in Mexico.

I couldn't believe I actually felt that way, but I did. I knew that was why I hadn't put our house on the market yet. And I knew that was why we hadn't gotten our own place in Cavendish...why we were still living in Jessica's basement.

"Kelly's signing up for Lamaze classes," Laci told me one day and I sighed.

"Don't worry," she went on. "You don't have to go."

Good.

"I'm going though," she said. "I'm going to be her Lamaze coach."

Of course you are.

"She wants both of us to be there when the baby's born. You'll see, David. This is going to be good. It's going to make all the difference when we actually see him for the first time."

I hoped she was right.

In the meantime, Starr set up a meeting with the baby's father. His name was Wade and it was obvious that he didn't want to have anything to do with us or with the baby. I wasn't sure how Kelly had even talked him into coming to the meeting.

"Are you going to want any visitation with the child?" Starr asked him.

"No."

"Would you like to receive letters, photos, things of that nature as the child grows?"

"No."

"Would you be willing to sign all necessary documentation terminating your parental rights?"

"I'll sign 'em right now," he said.

"We can't do that until the baby is actually born," Starr told him.

"Okay."

"He's not that bad," Kelly told us when we were alone. "He just doesn't want to be a father right now. He's supposed to go to college this fall...a baby's not what he wants right now."

Maybe he should have thought of that a few months ago.

Kelly was changing. Every time Laci visited with her, she would report back to me something Kelly had said or done or asked.

We knew that God was working in her life and drawing her closer to Him, and I knew that Laci was playing a big part in that. No one could have shown God's love to Kelly the way Laci was doing.

But finally I realized that God was trying to draw *me* closer to Him too. There'd been times when I'd thought I was "there" – at a place in my life where I was sure I was doing everything that God wanted me to do and that I couldn't get any closer to Him.

Now I was discovering that no matter who you are...no matter how close to God you think you might be...there's always further to go.

More than once I thought I'd completely forgiven Kyle. The first time was when I'd gone to visit him in prison. That had been a big step. But then Kyle had asked me about Greg and I hadn't been able to talk with him about it. If I'd truly forgiven Kyle, then that wouldn't have been a problem.

Later, once I'd been able to share with Kyle all about Greg, I thought I'd really forgiven him...and after that I'd even attended his execution. I hadn't gone because I wanted to see him die...I went because I wanted him to know that I loved him.

That was it, right? Wasn't that the ultimate in forgiveness?

But now I understood that if I'd truly forgiven Kyle I wouldn't have any hesitation about adopting his nephew. I would have let Stephen have the middle name Paul or even David (which was another one I'd nixed). I would have loved him already and I would have felt truly thankful to God for bringing him and Kelly into our lives.

I asked myself how I would feel if God would only forgive me as much as I'd been able to forgive Kyle.

And I knew the answer.

I wouldn't feel very good at all.

Jessica invited Kelly over for dinner. I told Jessica to find a sitter for the kids.

"Why?"

"Because, I don't think we need Cassidy patting her tummy and learning that her new little cousin's in there and then having Kelly change her mind. Cassidy's already lost one cousin."

"Kelly's not going to do that," said Laci, who was listening.

"Cassidy's *not* meeting Kelly until the baby's born and the paperwork's signed," I insisted.

Jessica went ahead and got a sitter.

The night Kelly came over for dinner I made an effort to be extra friendly to her. I kept thinking that this was the first of many "family" meals we'd all be sharing together. I knew that for every birthday party Stephen had, for every Christmas, for every mother's day, Kelly was going to be there. I think I was having as hard of a time with that as I was with the fact that Stephen was Kyle's nephew.

I was trying – *really trying* – to have a good attitude about all of it.

After dinner we went into the living room. Jessica had made chocolate chip cookies and we were eating them. I went back into the kitchen to grab seconds and to get some milk when I heard a commotion from the living room. I stepped into the doorway to see what was going on.

Jessica and Laci were both sitting one either side of Kelly, their hands pressed against her belly.

"There he goes again!" Jessica said. "Did you feel it?"

"Yeah," Laci said, smiling. She looked up and saw me standing in the doorway.

"Come here and feel this, David!"

I shook my head at her.

"It's okay if you want to," Kelly said quietly and I felt like if I didn't I was going to hurt her feelings so I walked over there and put my hand on her belly. I think it was the first time I'd ever touched her.

It seemed to take forever for him to move again. Jessica got up off the couch so I could sit down next to Kelly.

Finally I felt him move – nothing big – just a little jab with his fist or foot. I remembered all the times I'd felt Gabby do the same thing.

Hey there Gabby! Hey little girl! What are you doing in there? Are you going to be perfect like your daddy?

"Did you feel that?" Laci asked me. She still had her hand on Kelly's belly too.

I nodded and Laci smiled at me. Then he kicked again and for the first time I pictured him as the innocent little baby that he was.

After that, things got...*better*. Not great, but better. Kelly still acted like a dog who was about to get beat whenever I was around and Laci and I still wanted to go back to Mexico and adopt from our orphanage, but God was beginning to bring us a real peace about everything.

There's no way that I loved Stephen like I'd loved Gabby...

But it wasn't totally out of the question that one day I might.

Mrs. White wanted us to come over for dinner and bring Kelly too. As hard as Laci tried though, she couldn't convince Kelly to come...so Laci and I went by ourselves. I figured that if Kelly wanted her baby to be a part of our family then she'd better start getting used to being around Mrs. White and Charlotte.

"No lasagna?" I asked when I saw that the grill was going on the back deck.

"Sorry," Mrs. White told me. "I don't heat up the oven a lot during the summer...I guess I should have remembered. I could give Laci the recipe."

"Yeah, right!" I scoffed.

"What?!" Laci asked.

"I'm not even sure if she can cook," I whispered to Mrs. White.

"I can cook!" Laci argued.

"Well," I said, "I wouldn't know. I've been either eating at the orphanage or in Jessica's kitchen ever since we got married."

"I help Jessica *all the time*!" Laci protested.

"Yeah," I said. "Cassidy 'helps' her all the time too and I know for a fact that Jessica gets a lot more done when Cassidy's watching TV."

Laci swatted me.

"I'll give you the recipe and you can prove him wrong, okay?" Mrs. White told her, laughing.

"I wouldn't make him lasagna if he dropped down on his knees and begged me," Laci said, sticking her chin in the air.

"Give me the recipe," I said. "I'll make it myself."

"Oh! I'm sure that would turn out great," Laci scoffed.

"You two should have a contest!" Charlotte suggested, carrying a pan of marinating steaks to the deck.

"I'm game if you are," Laci told me.

"What do I get if I win?" I asked, pulling her toward me.

"You've already got me," she said, wrapping an arm around my waist. "What else could you *possibly* want?"

"Nothing," I said, kissing her.

"Good answer," Mrs. White said and Laci smiled at me.

She smiled more and more now. They weren't the big, broad smiles that I used to see all the time, but I'd take what I could get.

"Ready for tenth grade?" Laci asked Charlotte over dinner.

"I can't wait!"

"What math are you taking?" I wanted to know.

"Honors Algebra Two."

"That's my girl," I said. Maybe if she and Jordan did wind up getting married one day their kids would at least have one parent who could help them do their math.

Charlotte and Laci offered to do the dishes after dinner so Mrs. White and I went out onto the deck.

"How much longer before Stephen's due? About six more weeks?" she asked.

"Uh-huh," I nodded.

"You two have everything that you need?"

"Pretty much."

She paused. Then she spoke quietly.

"How hard is it?"

"Pretty hard," I admitted. "It's getting better, but it's been hard."

"I don't know if I could do it," she said, shaking her head.

"Yes, you could," I smiled. She'd always been about five steps ahead of me when it came to obeying God.

"Maybe," she smiled back. "Is there anything I can do for you?"

"Just pray," I said. "I really want to love him without any reservations and I know that's not going to happen until I've *completely* forgiven Kyle. Just pray for me...and for Laci too."

"I already have been."

"I know."

We decided to have our lasagna bake-off the next week. Since we'd be making so much lasagna we invited Laci's mom and dad, my mom and dad, Mrs. White, and Charlotte.

I'd invited Mike and Tanner too, but Mike was taking summer classes and couldn't make it home from school. Tanner wasn't able to come either because the high school football team was attending a week-long training camp at State. Laci invited Natalie and Ashlyn. Natalie couldn't make it all the way from Denver just for some lasagna, but Ashlyn said that she and Brent would definitely be there.

We dubbed it the "First Annual Lasagna Bake–Off" and I was okay with that. I figured that if Kelly *did* change her mind and we moved back to Mexico that it would be a good excuse for us to come back to Cavendish every August.

I may have cheated a little because I called Greg's grandmother down in Florida and got her recipe. That probably would have worked out really well for me if I'd known how to actually boil noodles or how to brown ground beef, but I didn't and Laci's lasagna won hands down.

Secretly I was relieved that one of us knew how to cook. We were going to have to move out of Jessica's pretty soon and had started looking for a place of our own.

Just to rent though. A place of our own to *rent*.

I wasn't quite ready to buy.

Mike called me one morning the week after our lasagna bake-off...about four weeks before Stephen was due. He was in town and he wanted to see us that night.

"He said he has a surprise," I told Laci.

"A surprise?"

"Uh-huh."

"I wonder what it is?"

"I bet it's a girl," I said. "I bet he's engaged or something."

"Really?"

"Yup."

"Why do you think that?"

"He wants to meet us at *Chez Condrez*," I said.

"So?" she said.

"So," I said, trying to act serious. "It's a *very* romantic place."

"I wouldn't know," she said dryly. "I've never been there."

"I have!" I said, grinning.

"Don't remind me."

"I was there with the wrong girl though," I said, pulling her to me. "I'd rather go with you."

She smiled at me.

"Jessica was no fun," I told her.

"Jessica?"

"Yeah...our parents took us there for her sixteenth birthday. Why? Who'd *you* think I was talking about?"

She raised an eyebrow at me.

"Oh, yeah! *Sam!* I'd almost forgotten all about her! Okay, now Sam was fun!"

Laci glared at me.

"I'd still rather take you though," I smiled and then I added, "I figure I'll probably get a whole lot further with you tonight than I did with her."

"Don't count on it," Laci said.

When we arrived at the restaurant the hostess told us that the rest of our party had already been seated so we followed her through the restaurant as she weaved toward a back table.

I'd been right. Mike was sitting there with a young woman. He grinned (and I think blushed) when he saw us and they both stood up to meet us.

"Hi, Mike," Laci said, hugging him.

"Hi, Laci," he said, hugging her back for a long moment. While they were hugging I looked at the woman. No, actually I looked at the woman's hands. I was trying to spot evidence of a *typical* engagement.

At first I was disappointed because around her ring finger was a silver band with writing on it. It was definitely *not* an engagement ring. Then I felt my own ring and I realized I was looking at her wrong hand. On her left hand I saw the diamond ring.

I knew it.

By now Mike was finished hugging Laci and he saw me checking out his fiancé's hand. He had a very impish look on his face as we shook hands and pounded each other on the back.

"Hi, Dave."

"Hi, Mike," I said, trying not to laugh at him. "So what's new?"

"I want you to meet someone," he said. "Laci, David...this is Danica."

"Hi, Danica," Laci said, shaking her hand. I did the same.

"Hi," I said. "It's nice to meet you."

"You too," she said to us. "Mike has told me *so* much about both of you."

"Gee, that's funny," I said, glancing at Mike, "he hasn't told us *anything* about you..."

He was definitely blushing now.

"So, Mike," I said. "I've been very excited about your surprise. What is it? I just can't imagine..."

Laci elbowed me.

"Danica and I are getting married," he said, taking her hand and holding it up so that we could see the ring. Laci squealed.

Why do they always do that?

There was another round of hugs and this time Danica was included.

"So what do you do?" Laci asked her after we'd sat down.

"I'm doing my residency in psychiatry," she said.

"You're going to be a psychiatrist?" I asked her and she nodded. "That's good. It'll come in handy if you're going to marry Mike."

He smirked at me and Danica laughed.

"See, Danica," he said, "didn't I tell you that David was just *great*?"

She laughed again.

While we were eating our salads I watched Danica and I watched how she and Mike interacted with each other. Before the main course arrived she and Laci went to the ladies' room. By then I'd already made up my mind about her.

"Well?" Mike asked as soon as they were gone.

"I can't believe you were able to talk someone into marrying you...much less her."

"Come on," he said. "Seriously. Whatdya think?"

"I think she's great."

"Really?"

"Yeah," I said, nodding. "Really. I think she's perfect for you. Laci likes her too...I can tell."

He smiled and looked relieved.

"Did you guys have classes together or something?"

"No," he said. "She's three years ahead of me..."

"How'd you meet?"

"Well," he said, glancing down for a moment. "Remember when you kept calling me about Laci and asking me about her medicines and stuff?"

I nodded.

“Well, every time you had a question I’d go and ask Dr. Jacobs about it in the psychiatry department. Danica was working in his research lab and I saw her almost every time I went down there.”

“I don’t remember asking you *that* many questions.”

“Well,” he said, grinning, “I wanted to be thorough...”

“Especially after you met her I suppose?”

“Uh-huh.”

“Glad I could help,” I said, smiling back.

Over dinner we started talking about Stephen. Since we had a psychiatrist sitting at the table I decided to ask her about Stephen and his biological background. I’d already looked up a bunch of stuff online, but I figured it wouldn’t hurt to ask some specific questions. I was pretty sure that Mike had filled her in on everything.

“I know that things like schizophrenia can have a genetic component,” I said. “How likely do you think it is that Stephen’s going to have the some kind of problem based on his family history?”

“Based on the fact that his uncle tried to kill himself or that he actually killed two people?”

“Both,” I said. “And Kyle’s dad killed himself...so that’s Stephen’s grandfather. Plus I’m not sure how stable the mother is...”

Laci shot me a look.

“Well, I’m not, Laci. If she and Kyle were just messed up because of the way they were raised or something, that’s one thing, but I’m worried that there’s more to it than that. I really don’t want to wake up seventeen years from now in the middle of the night to find Stephen bludgeoning us or something.”

Mike leaned toward Danica.

“David’s a bit of a pessimist,” he whispered loudly, smiling at me.

“I didn’t know that Kyle’s dad killed himself,” Danica said. “How old was Kyle when that happened?”

"Eleven or twelve, I think," I said and Laci nodded.

"You know," Danica said, shaking her head, "it's pretty hard to have something like that happen at that age and *not* get messed up. I don't suppose either one of them had any counseling after that?"

We both shook our heads.

"What was Kyle like when you visited with him in prison?"

"He was very remorseful," Laci said.

"And very worried about how what he'd done was affecting everybody else," I added.

"And he accepted Christ before he died, right?" Danica asked.

We both nodded again.

"He was actually praying for all of us," Laci said, "that what he'd done wouldn't cause any of us to stumble."

"What about Kelly?" Danica wanted to know.

"That's a different story..." I said.

"What's she like?"

"Well," Laci began, "she wants more for Stephen than what she and Kyle had and she doesn't think she can give it to him."

"Can she?" Danica asked.

"She wants what's best for him. She's doing a lot of stuff right now only because she wants to do what's right."

"Like what?"

"I know she's taking all her vitamins and she's going to her doctors appointments..."

"Big deal, Laci," I said. "That doesn't mean she'd be a good mother."

"There's more," Laci went on. "She wants this baby to be saved like Kyle was. She's been praying for him with me. It's not something she's comfortable with, but it was her idea. She really, *really* wants him to know Christ. I think that's becoming the most important thing to her. She really loves this baby."

"But she doesn't know Christ?" Danica asked.

"She hasn't accepted Him," Laci said. "I don't think she believes He can love her. I think she really wants His love, but she won't allow herself to feel it."

"What about Stephen's father? Have you met him?"

"Yeah," I nodded. "He's just a kid who wishes he could go back and do things differently."

"What about Kelly's mother?" Danica asked.

"Kelly still lives with her...she doesn't want to, but she's only sixteen...she doesn't have much choice. Kelly said she drinks all the time...pretty much stays drunk. Always has, ever since the dad killed himself."

Danica paused for a moment and then looked at me.

"The fact that both Kyle and Kelly have had the capacity to love and care deeply about people other than themselves is really important. It sounds like medically Stephen's greatest risks are going to be for depression and alcoholism. Both of those can have a genetic component, but it doesn't sound like there's anything else going on there that would be genetic."

"*Alcoholism and depression?*" Laci asked.

"Yes," Danica said, "but even though they can both have a genetic aspect, his environment is going to play a huge factor...*huge*. I think his environment is going to greatly outweigh anything else that's going on."

"So you don't think David's going to wake up with a knife in his back one day?" Laci asked with a smile.

"Not unless you put it there."

"That's why I always sleep with my eyes open," I said.

Over dessert, Mike asked us if we were going to have a baby shower for Stephen.

"No," we both answered at the same time and Laci looked down at her dessert.

"We pretty much have everything that we need," I said quietly.

Danica put her hand on Laci's.

"I heard about Gabby," she said. "I'm very sorry."

I was pleased that Danica knew Gabby's name.

It made me like her even more.

"I *love* Danica," Laci said as soon as we got into the car. "Didn't you love her?"

"She's great," I agreed. "Now all we gotta do is get Tanner married off..."

"And Natalie..."

We looked at each other.

"Hmmm..." Laci said (as if she had never thought of *that* before).

"Anyway," I said, "I'm happy for him. Of course I'm even happier for me..."

"Why?"

"Because I got to go to *Chez Condrez* for dinner and now I'm getting to go home with you..."

She smiled at me and shook her head.

"You still think you've got a chance tonight...don't you?"

I was glad that I'd asked Danica about Stephen. That had really been the only thing I was still concerned about and now I wasn't worried at all. I think I already knew everything that she'd told me, but hearing her confirm it made me feel really good.

Did I love Stephen yet?

Maybe not quite...but I was getting close.

I knew it was coming.

We found a house to rent about three blocks from our church. Two weeks before Kelly was due we paid the first month's rent and a $1,000 non-refundable deposit.

When we'd been pregnant with Gabby my mom had gone kind of crazy and bought an entire set of nursery stuff for the times we were home. Now my dad and I took all of it out of their attic and set it up in the Stephen's room.

Laci's parents gave us her old double bed. They also told us that they'd really been meaning to get a new dining room set and that we could have their old one. Then my mom and dad suddenly decided that they wanted a new couch so we took theirs.

All the office stuff that we'd used in Jessica's basement I had bought back when we'd first stayed there before Gabby was born. I set it all back up in the third bedroom, but I didn't decorate the walls.

The Saturday after we'd moved in, Tanner showed up at our door.

"I'm here for the lasagna," he said.

"You're about three weeks too late."

"Well, then," he said, "I'm here to help you move."

"You're about two days too late for that."

"Are you sure?" He looked at his watch.

"Positive," I said. "But I'm putting together an entertainment center and you're *more* than welcome to help me with that."

"Great," he said, rolling his eyes.

A few minutes later he was as frustrated with the instructions as I was and we decided just to try and do what seemed to make sense.

"Where's Laci?" he asked, holding up what appeared to be a drawer front.

"Spending the day with Kelly."

"So this 'Kelly' is going to basically be a part of your lives for the next eighteen years after you get Stephen?"

"I guess so," I sighed.

"Isn't that going to be kind of weird?"

"Yeah."

"Is she...nice?"

"She's quiet. She acts like she thinks I hate her though."

"Do you?"

"No," I said. "I may resent her a bit..."

"Why? Because she's Kyle's sister?"

"Maybe a little, but mostly I think it's because she's keeping us from going back to Mexico."

"I thought you hated Mexico."

"I never said I hated Mexico."

"Yeah...you pretty much said you hated Mexico."

"Well," I said, "I don't hate it now and I want to go back. Maybe I never thought I'd be saying that, but it's true."

"Why? Why do you want to go back?"

"Mostly because Laci wants to go back there so much. All she's ever wanted to do is work down there and help those kids. It's just about killing her to have to stay here."

"What else?"

I rifled through a bag of screws and looked for one that might possibly secure a side panel to the drawer front he was holding. I didn't answer him.

"What else?" he asked again.

"I guess I sort of liked helping the kids too," I finally said.

"It's that Dorito kid, isn't it?" Tanner asked.

I looked at him, surprised.

"What makes you say that?"

"Because," he said, shrugging. "I've known you forever. I can tell when you really like someone. I knew you liked Laci before *you* knew you liked Laci."

"Yeah," I said, narrowing my eyes at him. "*That's* why you took her to the prom."

"Well," he said, grinning. "I was really just trying to help."

"Uh-huh."

"Seriously. I figured one of two things was going to happen...either you'd realize that you liked her or she'd realize that she liked me."

I threw a drawer handle at him.

"You can't blame a guy for trying," he said, still smiling.

When Laci got back the entertainment center was finished, Tanner had gone home, and I was sitting on the couch looking at the album Charlotte had given us our first Christmas in Mexico. Laci flopped down next to me.

"How'd it go with Kelly today?"

"Good," she said. "How was your day?"

"Good." I pointed at the entertainment center.

"It looks nice," she said. "Is it going to collapse if we actually put a TV on it though?"

"If it does we'll blame it on Tanner," I said. "He helped me."

"How's he doing?"

"Okay I guess. He asked me if I'd help Jordan again this fall," I said, turning another page.

"What'd you tell him?"

"I told him if we were still here I'd be glad to."

"I think we're going to still be here," she said. "I think you need to go ahead and start planning along those lines."

"Not until all the paperwork's signed," I said firmly. "Kelly could still change her mind."

"About what?"

"About us having to stay here. Maybe she's going to decide that she doesn't ever want to see the baby again. Maybe she'll decide that it'll be too painful and that it'll be easier just to sever all ties with him."

"I really don't think that's going to happen."

"Well, maybe she'll decide she can't part with him at all and she won't let us adopt him."

"That's what you really want, isn't it?" she asked quietly. She didn't say it in a mean way or like she was upset. She just said it like she wanted to know.

"What I really want is for us to be able to be happy," I told her, "no matter what happens."

"We will," she promised, resting her head on my shoulder and looking down at the album.

We flipped on through the pages and came to the section with the letters from all of our friends. We looked at Greg's page for a very long time and then we turned to the end where Charlotte had left the blank pages for us to add things about Gabby.

There was her birth certificate with her little footprints on it and a tiny plastic bag with a lock of her hair. The rest of the pages were still empty.

We stared at that page for a long time too, just sitting quietly and looking at it. Laci ran her finger back and forth across the little bag.

"We're going to put Stephen's stuff right here," I finally said, touching the first blank page.

"Okay," she nodded, and then we closed the book.

The call from Kelly came in the middle of the night a day before she was due. Laci answered the phone and told her we'd be right there.

I'd been to Kelly's house before, but never inside. I'd always either picked her up or dropped her off outside. She'd never seemed to want me to go in.

I was about to find out why.

Laci turned to me just before we let ourselves in.

"Kelly's hasn't had the energy to do much lately," Laci said. "Usually she tries really hard to take care of her mother and clean up and stuff..."

"Okay."

"I just...I just don't want you to be shocked..."

That warning did no good...I was shocked. Every negative image that might come to your mind when you think of what a drunk's house might look like will probably not do justice to what I found when I entered that house. It was *awful*.

It smelled like garbage. There were dirty dishes covering every available surface and there were empty liquor and wine bottles littering the floor.

Laci went down the hall, presumably into Kelly's bedroom, and I could hear them talking to each other. I stayed in the living room and looked at a picture that was hanging askew on the wall.

It was of the Dunn family...taken before their father had killed himself. They all looked so happy, so...*normal*. I looked into the eyes of the father, searching for the answer as to what could have gone wrong and set such a terrible chain of events into motion. They just smiled back at me, saying nothing.

Kelly and Laci finally emerged from the bedroom and Kelly was startled to see me. She seemed horrified that I was seeing the inside of her house, plus she was probably scared to death about what was getting ready to happen.

We helped her into the car and Laci sat in the back with her while I drove.

"Is it bad?" Laci asked.

"Well," Kelly said softly, "it's bearable right now, but this is early on...right? I don't know if I'm going to be able to take it if it's a whole lot worse."

"If it gets bad you'll just get an epidural," Laci assured her.

"But what about the baby?" she cried. "I don't want to do anything that'll hurt the baby."

"Kelly," Laci said, "you know they're not going to give you anything that's going to hurt the baby."

"But it's better for the baby if you don't have anything," Kelly said, starting to sob. "I just want to do what's best for the baby!"

"I know you do," Laci said, trying to sooth her, but Kelly kept crying. I drove faster.

We arrived at the hospital and got Kelly all checked in. She walked into her room with Laci at her side. I wasn't sure, but I had the eerie feeling that it was the same room that Gabby had been born in. Probably not though. Don't they all look the same?

"Are you going to be in here for the birth?" the nurse asked me.

"Ummm," I wasn't really sure what to say.

"Yes," Kelly said, surprisingly loud. Then more quietly she said to me: "If you want."

I nodded at her.

The doctor came by, checked Kelly, and informed us that it was going to be a while. That turned out to be an understatement. I called our parents at seven in the morning and they spent the *entire day* in the lobby. It was after ten o'clock that night before the doctor told Kelly she could finally start pushing.

She didn't take one thing for pain the whole time.

Stephen was born one minute after midnight. I think he'd been waiting until his actual due date to arrive. In contrast to Gabby's birth, it was very, very loud in the room when he was born. Most of the noise came from Stephen who was howling and crying at the top of his lungs.

They wiped him off hurriedly and pretty soon he was all swaddled up and a nurse walked over to Kelly with him. The nurse started to hand him to her, but Kelly shook her head and pointed at Laci. Then she started crying.

The nurse handed the baby to Laci, but Laci didn't hold him too long because Kelly was crying so hard. She handed him to me and took Kelly's hand, talking to her softly.

I looked down into Stephen's face. Many times I had tried to imagine what I would feel when I saw him for the first time or what I would think. Usually I pictured myself feeling resentful or angry or sad. I'd tried often to see myself as happy or elated or thrilled.

The reality was that all I saw was a little baby boy and he didn't remind me of Gabby or Kyle or Greg or even his mother.

He was just Stephen.

Kelly was going to get to spend all of Stephen's birthday in the hospital and then be released the following day. We went home for a few hours to sleep after Kelly had promised Laci that she'd be okay by herself. I think she was sound asleep before we left the room.

The next day we visited for about two hours in the morning and then again in the afternoon. Kelly got up and took a walk around the ward with Jessica – I think so that we could be alone with Stephen for a little while.

"What do you think?" Laci asked after they were gone.

"I think it's going to be really good," I said, looking down at Stephen who was lying on my lap, his head at my knees.

"You do?" She looked at me to see if I meant it.

I did.

"I didn't think I'd be able to love him," I told her, "but you were right."

"I think it's going to be good too," she said. I glanced back at her and she was smiling at me.

"You know," I warned Laci, wrapping Stephen's hand around my finger and stroking it with my thumb, "she can still change her mind."

"I know," Laci said. "I'm not getting too attached."

"Yeah, right."

"Well," she admitted, smiling and reaching a hand over to him to stroke his hair, "I'm attached, but you know what I mean. If she decides to keep him...it would be hard, but I'd be okay."

"Do you think she will?"

"You saw where she's living," Laci said, shaking her head. "Even if she wanted to, I don't see how she can."

That night we went into the nursery and stood by the empty crib, just looking.

“We still haven’t picked a middle name,” Laci reminded me.

“Maybe something will come to us by tomorrow.”

“I hope so,” Laci said. She wound up the mobile over his bed and we listened to it play for a minute before we turned out the light and left the room.

We walked into Kelly's room the next morning and found her sitting up in bed. What stopped me in my tracks was that Wade was sitting next to her, holding Stephen.

I looked at Laci and squeezed her hand. I was suddenly worried about her because I *knew* what was coming and I could tell by the look on Laci's face that she knew too.

Kelly started crying as soon as she saw us and Wade had to do most of the talking. I didn't catch all the details, but the gist of it was that Kelly was going to move into his parent's house and he was going to attend the local community college. They were also going to get married.

After he finished Kelly managed to choke out a sentence. She wanted to know if we'd ever be able to forgive her.

"Kelly," Laci said, taking her hand. "There's nothing to forgive. This is *your* baby...you have every right to keep him. You know that...we've talked about that."

"Will you pray with me?" Kelly asked her. "One more time?"

"We both will," Laci said and she reached for my hand.

We had just walked out of the room when I suddenly realized that I needed to ask Kelly something.

Wade was leaning over Kelly, their foreheads touching. Both of them were smiling down at their baby.

"I'm sorry to bother you," I said and Wade straightened up.

"It's okay," Kelly said softly.

"I just...I wanted to know what his name is. Did you decide on a name?"

"Oh," Kelly said, smiling slightly and looking up at Wade. "We're going to call him Stephen. Stephen Wade..."

Now I knew why Laci and I hadn't been able to pick a middle name before. We'd never tried Wade.

"I like that," I told her. "It's perfect."

Kelly smiled at me and I went back out into the hall where Laci was waiting.

When we got to the parking lot I stopped and pulled Laci tight against me.

"Are you okay?" I whispered. I felt her nod against my shoulder.

"Are you sure?" I asked, pulling back and looking at her. There were tears in her eyes but she did seem alright.

"I'm sure," she said, nodding again. "I knew all along this was about more than just God giving us a baby."

"You did really good, Laci," I told her. "No one could have done more for her than what you did."

She nodded slightly and wiped a tear away. We got into the car and I held her hand the whole way home. It was a very quiet ride.

As soon as we got back to the house I went out into the backyard and started making phone calls. When I was done I found Laci in the bedroom and pulled her to me.

"Can you be ready to go home in eight days?" I asked her.

She nodded and a smile tugged at her lips.

"I talked to Inez about starting the paperwork," I said. And then, just in case she didn't know what I meant, I added, "for us to adopt."

A huge, broad smile spread across her face and I thought how I hadn't seen that smile in such a long time.

"Dorito's still there," I went on. "Inez said he's all ours."

Suddenly the smile was gone.

"What's the matter?"

"Nothing," she said, hesitating. "I just..."

"We *have* to get Dorito, Laci...we just *have* to!"

"Right," she said, nodding and trying unsuccessfully to smile again.

"What's wrong? I thought you'd be so happy."

"I am," she insisted. "I am."

"No, you're not. What's wrong?"

"Nothing...I just..." She shook her head.

"You just *what*?" I persisted.

"I just thought we'd get a *baby*," she finally said softly. Then, more forcefully, "but it's fine and you're right. You're absolutely right – we have to get Dorito."

"Laci," I said, starting to laugh. "I didn't mean we couldn't get a baby too...he's going to need little brothers and sisters!"

"Really?"

"Of course, really," I said.

"Brothers *and* sisters?" she asked. "Plural?"

"All you want," I nodded.

She flung her arms around me.

“There’s just one thing though,” I said and she pulled back to look at me.

“What?”

“*Tienes que mantenerlos fuera de mi oficia.*”

You’ve got to keep them out of my office.

The smile returned to her face one more time and she nodded at me before she laid her head against my chest and squeezed me tight.

Available **Now** On Amazon:

Book One: *Chop, Chop*
Book Two: *Day-Day*
Book Three: *Pon-Pon*

Also available at Target.com

Coming Soon:

Book Four: *The Other Brother*
Book Five: *The Other Mothers*
Book Six: *Gone*
Book Seven: *Alone*

For more information and free downloadable lesson plans, be sure to visit: www.LNCronk.com

Ordering five or more copies of any of the *Chop, Chop* books? Save over 50% off the retail price **and receive free shipping!**

For details, visit www.LNCronk.com or send an email to: info@LNCronk.com.

While the concept of forgiveness is appreciated by people from religions and nations throughout the world, the reality that Jesus Christ loved us enough to die for the forgiveness of our sins is not.

If you enjoyed *Chop, Chop* and feel others would benefit from its important message, please consider doing one or more of the following:

- Word of mouth is one of the most powerful tools you have available...***tell others about it!***
- Give *Chop, Chop* as a gift.
- Make sure your local library has a copy of *Chop, Chop*. If they don't, ask them to order a copy for their patrons.
- Write a book review for your local paper, favorite magazine, or websites such as www.goodreads.com or www.Amazon.com.
- If you know someone in the media (newspaper, radio, TV or Internet) tell them about *Chop, Chop* and ask them to read and review it.
- Visit www.LNCronk.com for details on how to request a free set of *Chop, Chop* bookmarks to help spread the word.
- Consider donating one or more copies of *Chop, Chop* to your church library or school library.
- If you have a website, post a link to www.LNCronk.com.
- *Chop, Chop* is excellent for Sunday schools, Bible studies, home schools and other types of Christian education. Leaders can find free, downloadable lessons (many of which are stand-alone lessons that are not dependant upon the novel) at www.LNCronk.com.
- Order multiple copies of *Chop, Chop* at over 50% off the list price for educational purposes or for resale and receive free shipping. For details, visit the website or send an email to: info@LNCronk.com.

Made in the USA